# Danger Beyond The Yellow Gate

## By: Cathy Henn

# Danger Beyond The Yellow Gate

©2017 Cathy Henn

Available for purchase at:
www.createspace.com/7091289

ISBN-13: 978-1548142070

The cover illustration was created by Kyle Henn.
Check out some of Kyle's designs at:
www.kylehenndesign.com

How to contact the author:

Cathy Henn

henncathy@gmail.com

## Acknowledgements

Many thanks to Lieutenants John and Harry who came over from *The Virgin and The Veteran* to chase Clyde through another book.

Thank you to my beloved husband, Karl (RawDog), for your love and support. You wrote all the best lines and came up with the title, so as usual, it is all your fault.

Thanks to my son, Kyle, for creating the incredible cover illustration.

A special thanks to Frozen Ed and Gail for your support and friendship.

Many thanks to RawDog, Frozen Ed, scRitch, Kyle, and Margaret for your advice and editing skills. Thanks to Danger, RawDog, laz, Frozen Ed, and scRitch for your stories.

This book is a work of fiction. Quotes and people's names are used with permission.

# Dedication

This book is dedicated to my marvelous granddaughter, Marcie, who is the heart of our family.

# Chapter 1: Coming Home

*Arrival at camp, Friday morning*

The steady beat of the techno music inside his truck cab was intoxicating. He bobbed his head up and down with the pulsating rhythm. The electronic funk got his mind in a sweet groove and lessened his worries about the upcoming misery and pain that awaited him out there in the mountains.

He was entered in a five loop race billed as the hardest 100-mile trail ultramarathon in the world, set in a hidden state park in the backwoods of Tennessee. The route wound in and out of hollers, up and down near vertical hills, and through every possible windfall and ravine. Most of the race was off-trail, which entailed beating through briar patches, plummeting down slippery slopes, and climbing up steep pitches and over downed trees. It was the masterpiece of a sadistic Race Director who enjoyed tormenting world class runners with the impossible. The race course had allowed less than twenty men to finish it in over thirty years of existence.

The long line of mountains was finally visible from his truck window. There was Frozen Head's peak in the distance, the valley where the old prison lay, then Indian Knob pointing up like a cone in the sky, then the long downhill slope of Kelly Mountain seeming to run right into the highway ahead.

As he rounded the bend where Kelly Mountain touched the road, he could see the valley where Beech Fork tumbled over its rocky bed in the distance and the flow of Chimney Top Mountain rolling away into the park.

There were places in those mountains affectionately nick-named by runners, given names that did not appear on any map, such names as The Bad Thing, Rat Jaw, Zipline, Vertical Smile, and Big Hell. He imagined his heart pumping in his throat as he climbed the Bad Thing, and he thought he felt the tentacles of Big Hell waiting to torture him.

As he drove around the hills even farther, he entered the road that led to the park. Directly in front of him was the prettiest view in the whole county: the row of blue and gray peaks on the horizon that formed the backdrop of the park. Bird Mountain and Chimney Top formed a deep V which encompassed Bald Knob to the left, with Squire Knob close by. Then the ridge line where the jeep road ran to Frozen Head rose and fell all the way to the right, with the top of Frozen Head hidden behind the right arm of the V.

## Danger Beyond The Yellow Gate

It was jarring that the county had chosen to build a correctional facility right in the middle of the valley, placed in front of the gorgeous view. Danger, aptly named by his college buddies for his love of taking risks, drove his truck past the sorry sight of men fenced in behind barbed wire. Some of them were working, digging holes and sanding wood, but many were lazily walking around or sitting on picnic tables. These were just the short-time criminals, though. The long-timers were shut in behind distant gray concrete walls of tall fortresses that only had slits for windows to the outside world.

The setting for the prison had a lot in common with the impossible ultramarathon he was about to run. When James Earl Ray failed in his escape from the old Brushy Mountain State Penitentiary, the seeds for the race were sown. Ray only lasted in the backwoods for less than 58 hours, and was found lost in the woods about eight miles from the prison. This became the impetus for the world's hardest ultramarathon, a cruel challenge of athletic ability, fortitude, spirit, and ego.

Danger knew he would be humbled by the race course before it was over. The challenge was even more formidable because he was not an ultrarunner or a record-breaking long distance hiker. He was merely someone who loved being out in the woods and hiking. He did have the advantage of having DNF'd (Did Not Finish) in the competition four times before, though, and he had been setting out the books that marked the route since he was eleven years old. He was pretty confident in his navigational skills. The race course itself was daunting, but by now he knew every peak, every stream, every ridgeline, and every boundary corner like the topography made by the knuckles, veins and bones on the back of his hand.

The runners did not know when the race would start each year, but it had to be between midnight Friday night and noon Saturday, at a time set by the Race Director's whim. A conch shell was blown to signify that the race would begin in one hour. They must run the same loop over and over five times, but sometimes loops were run clockwise and sometimes counterclockwise. Loops One, Two, and Three had to be finished in less than 13 hours and 20 minutes each, with no more than 40 hours total for finishing three loops. If a competitor managed to finish three loops, they had completed a "Fun Run." If a runner planned to do four or five loops, they had to do all the loops in less than 12 hours each. So the completion of all five iterations could take up to 60 hours.

## Danger Beyond The Yellow Gate

Running at night was slower, so competitors had to compensate for that. If a runner hoped to sleep, they had to run faster to make a cushion of time for rest.

There was no aid on the course except for two water drops and any aid runners brought for themselves in the campground where they passed through on every loop. Books had to be found which marked certain points on the course where runners were required to rip out a page to prove they had been there.

A briar-infested powerline hill near his house had been Danger's training plan for months. Running repeats on it and watching his diet had helped him to lose thirty pounds over the last year, and he was almost back to college weight. His truck was full of food and different packs full of essentials for each loop, including several sets of shoes and changes of socks, long pants, shorts, tights, jackets of different weights, rain gear, hats, gloves, water-purification tablets, hiking poles, duct tape, first aid, and everything else he could think of.

His big diesel pick-up truck roared as it took the turn into the park. He reached down to adjust his music and glanced at the dog collar hanging from his mirror. It was Flash's old red collar, a relic faded white now. He missed his friend who had been his favorite dog of all time. Black fur thick at the neck, but otherwise he had been similar to a black lab. Flash had been a great running companion, no matter the weather.

Runners never knew what the weather was going to be like during the race, as the area within the park seemed to have its own weather system. Sometimes the communities outside the park could be experiencing pretty spring-like weather, but the weather inside the park could be snowing and freezing cold. Or there could be sudden storms with high winds, horizontal sheets of sleet and rain, and raging floods of water rushing down the mountainsides. The days could be burning hot and the nights freezing cold. Runners had to try to prepare equally for all possibilities and impossibilities.

There could be thick fog on the mountaintops and down the hillsides. Danger thought night fog was the worst kind of fog because the fog reflected off your flashlight. All you could see was the glow right in front of you, so using a flashlight made visibility even more impossible.

It was entirely possible that he would run into snakes this year. The daytime temperatures had been high enough in the preceding weeks for the snakes to come out of their dens. The region's two venomous snakes, rattlesnakes and copperheads, were very common in these hills. He had a healthy respect for them, but not an irrational fear. There could also be herds of wild boar in the farthest reaches of the course, and maybe even a bear. The ticks would be out in hordes and biting for certain. Why God made ticks, he would never understand.

Recently, he had been hearing in the news that there had been mountain lion sightings in the county. That worried him some, considering he planned to be out on at least one night loop. He had read an online bit about what to do when encountering a mountain lion, and he thought there was no hope of escape without his hunting rifle.

He hoped his younger brother Bob was already in the park. Bob was going to be his in-camp aid crew this year. Danger was hoping to run more than one loop this time, so his little brother, who was not so little since he towered over him at 6'5", was essential to his performance. He wanted to show him his pile of gear and explain his plan for aid between loops before he rushed to set out one of the water drops for the race. He would have to empty out his truck into Bob's vehicle so he had room for the water jugs and the people who went with him to the backroads to take care of the water drop. He hoped Bob had already gotten the tent set up and space carved out for them at their family's campsite.

His mind drifted to thoughts of his wife and baby girl back home. His wife had encouraged him to go and try once more to finish this monster and get it out of his system. She was always like that, telling him, "You only live once; just go do it." Now he had to do it for her and for his little girl, so they would be proud of him. He hoped they would be able to come out to the course at least once and he would see them in camp. Spectators were only allowed at two places on the course: either up at the fire tower, or in the campground. They could only provide aid in the campground before the runner left out on a new loop. Once the runner touched the yellow gate and left the headquarters' area, no aid could be given anywhere on the course.

The weather was perfect, high in the 60's, with plenty of sunshine. He felt great, but as usual, he was starving. His stomach was always a bottomless pit. Maybe he could grab a package of peanut butter crackers before heading out to do the water drop. When he returned to camp, runners would be checking in at the race headquarters and getting their race numbers. Then the pre-race jitters would set in, as everyone huddled over the picnic table and anxiously marked their own maps with the correct route from the one official map.

Later, the chicken quarters would be roasting on the grill, digitally prepared by scRitch, the official Chicken Cook. The potluck meal would be coming together as people brought their offerings up to the headquarters' picnic table. Soon, he could eat all he wanted.

He was feeling hopeful about the race. It was going to be an incredible weekend full of surprises. He turned up the techno music full blast and rolled down the windows as he drove into the campground.

## Chapter 2: Friday Fun

*Friday afternoon and evening*

His pickup truck roared as he gunned it up the hill, and the computer-generated, metallic sounds of techno music pumped out his open window into the campground. People stopped what they were doing and looked up, surprised. His head was nodding in rhythm to the beat, his arm was on the windowsill, and his smiling face greeted the world.

He found his family at campsite 13, where they already had camp set up. They were waiting for him at the road, having heard his grand entrance. His Dad was smiling broadly under his mustache, and his Mom and sister-in-law Bibi were laughing. His brother Bob was bopping his head along with him to the music, saying, "Yeah!"

He backed his truck perfectly into the slot they had left him, and then he regretfully shut all the glorious sounds down and climbed out. Everyone hugged him, and other people came over to greet him.

"Hey Danger! Good to see you again, buddy!" His friend Frank shook his hand.

Frozen Ed was there with his wife, Gail. Danger held out his hand to greet him, but Ed grabbed him

## Danger Beyond The Yellow Gate

in a big hug, and so did Gail.

"Are you running this year, Ed?" he asked.

"Yeah, I'm back!" said the septuagenarian. "I've been training really hard all year, and this year I know just what to do! I will not fail!" Ed had been the very first person to finish the race many years ago. Almost every year since then, after failing to complete his goal of two loops, Ed swore he would not be back. But over the course of the year he changed his mind, and he came back to try again.

It was so good to be back with old friends and family. Danger felt really happy to be there preparing to run this incredible race once more, after many years of just being a spectator. Of course, he was also one of the group that set the books out every year to mark the checkpoints on the course, as well as being the bugler who blew *Taps* when someone quit the race, so he was always there in the background. Now his turn had come again to stand at the yellow gate with the other runners and give it his best shot.

"When do you want to do the water drop?" he asked his Dad, RawDog.

"Mom wants to go with us this time," said his Dad. "We're ready to go whenever you are."

"Okay, let me go up and see laz and check in, then I'll be ready," said Danger. He picked up the hefty metal belt buckle he had made to give to the first 24 hour finisher. He had made it in his metal-working class back in his college days, and it weighed about fifteen pounds.

He hurried up the hill, hoping he could get his race number this early. Lazarus Lake (laz), the Race Director, was there hanging up the license plates on ropes surrounding race headquarters. His collection expanded every year as first-time runners brought him a license plate from their home state or country.

"Hey, laz, how's it going?" Danger set his massive belt buckle down in its regular spot by the big tree. "Need any help?"

"Nah, everybody has already done everything. I like to hang these up myself to make sure it's done just right," said laz.

"I'm headed out to do the water drop. Any chance I can go ahead and check in?"

"Yeah, we can do that," said laz. They walked over to the picnic table, and laz got Danger's name written on the official list and gave him his race number and instructions.

## Danger Beyond The Yellow Gate

"When do I get my watch?" asked Danger. laz had banned everyone's fancy high-tech watches this year, and was passing out cheap watches with the time set to race time.

"Not until right before the start," grinned laz.

"Okay, well, I'll be back later. Mom and Dad are going with me."

He ran back down the hill to his truck, and his parents were both there, waiting, with their daypacks and jackets. His Dad was putting the old hog's skull tied onto a stick into the back of his truck; this was set up as a trail sign to mark Pighead Creek on the course. They climbed into his four door cab, Mom in the front seat and Dad in the back. He was glad to have some help, but wondered how much water they would be able to lug up the hill.

They stopped at the maintenance building and got the water jugs loaded into the back of the truck, and spent a few minutes shooting the bull with the Park Ranger. He told them about the hikers who had recently gotten stuck on the top in a winter storm and were experiencing signs of hypothermia. Rather than hike back down, they called 911. Word got to the park, and the rangers drove up the long jeep road to get them. They got there just in time to rescue them, as the hikers were in a bad way.

Danger drove the truck around the perimeter of the State Park on the old highway. They made a quick stop where Pighead Creek crossed under the road to set out the hog's skull to mark the way. Looking out the window was always interesting on this stretch of road. So much garbage pushed out the rear of trucks and thrown out windows for years and years had piled up all along the sides of the road and down into the gullies below the highway. There were torn-up couches, rusted-out washing machines, old toilets, a million plastic garbage bags and aluminum cans, and probably some stinking carcasses of dead animals. In fact, that was where they had found the rotting boar carcass one year and taken the skull to make the trail marker.

The concrete barrier on one section of the highway was covered in multi-colored sprays of paint. It made for a whole entertaining wall of graffiti. "Dawn loves TJ" and "TJ loves Dawn" were the sweet epithets of love painted by the local high school kids. He slowed down so they could look for new things painted on the wall. There were other bolder proclamations about Mike and Amber that made his Mom put her hand over her mouth and say, "Oh my!"

## Danger Beyond The Yellow Gate

"You know, on the highway from here to the jeep road, every road sign has an 'anatomy pictograph' painted on it," Danger told her.

His Dad gave out a loud, "*Hah!*" from the back seat, but his Mom laughed tentatively, as if she was unsure of his meaning.

They turned off the highway and drove up the bumpy jeep road past the oil wells and the overgrown old coal mining areas. Danger happily negotiated the water-filled muddy ruts in the road. His Mom held on tight to the sissy bar above the passenger door, and grimaced and groaned a bit when he suddenly dropped into a deep rut.

Finally, they arrived at the place to unload the water jugs. His Mom carried one in each hand cautiously up the muddy slope to the little flat place. He knew she was afraid of falling. His Dad followed with two jugs gripped in each hand. Danger grabbed four jugs in each hand and tromped up behind them. He dropped his jugs and his Mom rearranged them in tidy rows. Danger slid straight down the slope on his heels, but his Mom and Dad carefully picked their way down a side route. After about 20 minutes, Danger had taken the motherlode of jugs up the hill to the drop, and his Dad came in second place. His Mom had taken six jugs up in three trips, and she was tired. But he didn't mind. It was great to have them both along. He didn't get to spend much time with his parents now that he was married and had a child.

They drove back to the campground and walked up to the headquarters' area to greet old friends and new runners. Runners were huddled over the picnic table, peering at the one official map, intensely concentrating on marking their own maps with the line marking the course route. Danger already knew the route, so he didn't need to mark a map, but it was always best to double-check to make sure laz had not made any surprise changes. He looked down over Ed's head at the map, and matched the line on the map with the memory in his head, from start to finish, and then said, "Yep." The course was just as he knew it would be.

New runners had brought gifts to laz of comfy white socks, and other runners had brought other gifts of a more memorable nature. Chocolates, hot peppers, Canadian maple syrup, dog treats for his two dogs, chocolate cake, and six packs of off-brands of his favorite soda were all laid out on one end of the table. laz enjoyed the little perks of being the Race Director. It only cost $1.60 to enter the race, and the gifts, the fun, and the friendships made up for the lack of financial gain.

## Danger Beyond The Yellow Gate

A group of runners and family members were standing around near the fire, anxiously talking about the start time for the race. Danger saw Hiram there, and greeted him. The general consensus was that the start time was going to interfere with sleep this year.

"It's bound to be in the middle of the night," said Hiram. "Last year he said early starts allowed him to get home earlier on Monday."

"But last year's start was really early, so maybe this year he will make it a later time," said Danger. He knew a lot about the race, but he never knew the start time. Only laz and scRitch knew that.

"What time will the race start, scRitch?" someone hollered at scRitch, who was busily laying out chicken to cook on the grill.

scRitch stopped working, and looked at them from under the thick white hair that hung down in his eyes. "You believed all those stories that I know the start time? Me? Who we kiddin' here?" He was smiling and chuckling at the thought that he might have inside knowledge.

"But Keith said you know…," said Emily, who had just walked up. She was an attractive blonde returning for her second try at the race.

"Yeah, scRitch. You're supposed to know everything!" said Amanda, Emily's dark-haired friend who was also coming back for a second time.

"Is that Amanda? Emily?" Ed's head perked up at the picnic table where he had been slaving over his map. He pulled his legs out quickly from beneath the table and strode over to see them.

"Ed! So good to see you again!" Amanda and Emily took turns hugging him.

"I didn't think you girls would come back after our last little foray around the course!" said Ed. "Remember how you two had just met and were practically shoving each other out of the way to keep up with me?"

"Yeah, we had a little friendly competition going on last year. It was so much fun, we both decided to give it another try," said Emily.

"We will never forget all the things you taught us last year. And we figured you would be here, so we brought you and your wife presents," said Amanda.

"Oh, my, how nice of you," said Ed, accepting a big box of chocolate pecan candy from them. Ed loved chocolate and pecans.

"We remembered how much you liked bacon last

## Danger Beyond The Yellow Gate

time we ran with you, so we brought you some special bacon too," said Amanda. She handed him a package of maple syrup infused bacon.

"Wow!" he exclaimed. "I will have to cook this for tomorrow!"

"Maybe we can hang out with you during the race this year, too," said Emily.

"Maybe, maybe so," said Ed, eyes suddenly downcast.

Danger and Hiram were still standing nearby, and Ed introduced the girls to them. Others came over to discuss the route changes for this year's course.

"Hiram, I hear that you are the one we have to blame for all the course changes," said Pete, who was returning for his sixth time.

"Noooooo...not me. It was RawDog," said Hiram, smiling.

RawDog spoke up, saying, "It's always RawDog's fault. That's how it always is." He sounded morose, but he was only joking. He was used to everyone always blaming him for everything, when most of the time it was laz's fault.

Everyone laughed. Evening was coming on, and

most runners were checked in for the race now. People started bringing up items of food for the potluck meal, and the barbecued chicken was steaming on the grill. The chicken smelled delicious. scRitch turned over the pieces one last time, and said, "Coupla' more minutes and some people can eat."

The bystanders hurried to get paper plates and plastic ware so they would be first in line for the chicken. Some people went ahead and dug into potato salad, broccoli salad, bread, beans, and coleslaw.

The chicken was ready. scRitch served it straight from the grill to the lineup of runners, eager to finally taste his famous chicken. People sat at the table and in lawn chairs around the fire pit, enjoying the pre-race meal and the fellowship of comrades before an expedition. Someone had started a fire earlier, and it was putting out a nice amount of heat in the chill of the evening. The flames were reaching towards the sky in little bursts and flutters. Smoke was swirling upwards. Someone dumped a new log on the fire, and the smoke plummeted down from the sky and out into the crowd of people on one side of the fire. A couple of people had to jump up and move around to the other side of the fire pit to get away from the smoke.

## Danger Beyond The Yellow Gate

Danger was enjoying his pre-race meal. His chair was down at his family's campsite, so he squeezed in at the picnic table. He ate his chicken with his hands and used a spoon to shovel food into his mouth from his plate in between bites of chicken.

"Great job, scRitch!" he said loudly.

"Yeah! Delicious!" said someone else.

After everyone had eaten, the rumors of an early start caused most people to leave the campfire area and return to their own campsites to get to bed early. Some people were still not certain about what to bring in their packs, and a lot of repacking was going on. Little groups of people stood around on the road, worrying over the route changes, and discussing things like their race nutrition and the preparation of their feet to prevent blisters.

Danger wasn't worried about an early race start time. He and his wife had spent the last year and a half up every night with their baby, and he was used to running on empty. He decided to hang around the fire for a bit with some of his old friends and listen to the stories.

One of the best features of this race was the interesting cast of characters who came to run it. There were many scientists, engineers, mathematicians, teachers, preachers, writers, and other well-educated people who were attracted to this unusual event. It seemed to be a puzzle and a challenge that many smart people wanted to take up. The stories told by these people were always fun to listen to.

Ed was still at the campfire, although his wife had repeatedly told him to go to bed early. She had left for the motel for the night. Ed was obviously having too much fun to go to bed. scRitch was still there, cleaning up after his marathon cooking session. laz and RawDog were also there, and a few others were hanging around.

The campfire was the time-honored place for repeating the true and untrue stories of their race adventures. They were passed down from year to year, from runner to runner. Everyone loved the old stories.

scRitch unfolded a lawn chair, sat down, and began talking about some of his adventures out there in years past. He had a long history of almost 20 years coming to the race, and an even longer history as an ultrarunner going back nearly 25 years. In recent years, he had stopped trying to run the course, but still came back every year to visit and cook the chicken. It was his way of giving back. Plus he totally enjoyed the whole race atmosphere and seeing old friends.

scRitch was remembering Stu, who had died about a year ago. "I remember the time when I kept trying to stay ahead of Stu on the nonexistent trail. I would always stray somehow, which allowed him to catch up. He was just basically walking along, BUT…he knew the way! So, he would always catch me, and then sometimes he would scrape me! I swear, every single year he would say, 'People are gonna die out here! This time laz has gone too far!'"

There were a few chuckles from the others around the fire. scRitch kept on talking, remembering his old friend.

"He told me about the 'mystery of the mountains.' Something about some sort of spirits hovering around the park who would protect him. One time he was lost, and the spirits mystically guided him back to where he needed to be."

Danger had heard that story before. He thought about the possibility that there might be spirits out there to guide people. It was a strange idea.

"I bet you remember, RawDog, when I came back to camp that time and told you that there were in fact, TWO New Rivers. Remember? And another time I reported watching a creek actually flow UPHILL!"

"Yeah, I remember those stories," said RawDog, laughing.

laz joined in and said he always got a kick out of trying to imagine where scRitch would wander off to, and then listening to him telling his stories when he finally made it back.

Finally, Ed said he just had to get to bed, or Gail would fuss at him. He wandered off down the hill. Danger and his Dad followed him back to their shared campsite. After a quick trip to the restroom, Danger crawled into his tent, yawning. Everything was prepared for tomorrow. He was ready for a little shut-eye, and he hoped for a good night's sleep. Bob was ready to help him get going in the morning. He quickly texted his wife good night, then climbed into his sleeping bag and zipped it up. He fell asleep hearing the soft voices of mystical spirits hovering above his tent, talking about him.

## Loop One Begins

## Chapter 3: Time to Go

*Start of the race, Saturday 2:45 a.m.*

The short, hollow echo of the conch shell being blown didn't wake him, but his brother Bob poked him from outside the tent and said, "Hey, Danger, get up!" He moaned and pushed himself into a sitting position, instantly nervous and alert.

He hurried into his race clothes and shoes, while sitting inside the tent in the dark. So the scoundrel was going to start the race in the dark again, eh? That would scare some people, but not him. He had been training in the midnight hours for months. And there was a full moon this weekend, if the sky was clear enough to see it. At least he wasn't starting the race mid-morning, when everyone had been standing around waiting for hours, breakfast calories and adrenaline long gone and replaced by anger. An early morning start had some good points, but the darkness on the first loop could also kill many dreams of finishing five loops. Many ill-prepared runners would be lost as soon as they summited the first mountain, especially if it was foggy.

His brightest headlamp gripped his forehead through his orange knit hat, and his shoes were tied. He rolled out of the tent into the pre-dawn chilly air. Bob was doing his job with amazing efficiency, and had water boiling and ready for instant oats and hot chocolate. The tantalizing odor of frying bacon was coming from a skillet on the other burner of the camp stove. Danger rushed down the hill to the bathhouse and hurried back to a hot breakfast, which he shoveled into his mouth, followed by slugs of steaming chocolate. Several pieces of crunchy bacon followed, satisfying his need for fat and salt. Meanwhile, Bob was digging in the back of his Honda, and he set out Danger's first-loop pack, his hiking poles, and the bag full of essentials such as his map, compass, bib number, and everything else he had painstakingly prepared for the first loop.

Danger pocketed his most important things, anxiously tied his shoes a little bit tighter, pulled on his lightweight fleece jacket, said thanks to his brother Bob, hung his pack over one shoulder, and headed up to the yellow gate.

Runners were standing around in the road in front of the gate, shuffling from foot to foot, with gloved hands held in their armpits trying to warm them up. It was almost 2:45 a.m., one hour after the conch

## Danger Beyond The Yellow Gate

shell had called them out of their warm sleeping bags. Danger milled about, saying hey to old friends, and looking for someone to talk to. He saw his friend Frank and moved over to his side, smiling, but Frank was too nervous and jumpy to talk much. He saw Frozen Ed up at the gate, eager to be the first one to step onto the course when the cigarette was lit. laz always gave a few words of encouragement to the runners before the race began, but today all he said was, "Hurry."

Finally, it was time! The crowd of runners and spectators grew silent. Danger felt the rise and fall of his chest as his breathing quickened. He threw his fleece jacket to Bob and anchored his pack on his back and fastened its straps. His poles were ready in his hands and he was set to push off at the start.

A few straggling runners were still rushing to the gate when the last minute was breached, and the Race Director's cigarette was lit. Off they went up the jeep road to the mountains. Some of the entrants were speeding ahead, but not Danger. He was conserving his energy for later. Moving near the middle of the pack, he strode at a brisk walk. Frank was practically sprinting up the road near the front of the pack. Daniel had actually made it to the start in time, and was hurrying along in his yellow pants right behind Danger.

His mom and dad, and Bob and Bob's wife Bibi were all lined up on the rise by the side of the road, and yelling good luck to his back as he passed them by. They were screaming "bye!" over and over. He didn't yell back, as his mind was totally focused on the challenge ahead.

It took less than three minutes for all of the runners to leave camp at the start of the race, then the runners rounded the bend and all that could be seen of them was the glow of their headlamps weaving back and forth as they ascended the first mountain's switchbacks. The spectators and race staff stood around visiting for a few minutes, then some headed back to the comfort and warmth of their sleeping bags. After all, they wouldn't see any of the runners for at least six hours, unless someone quit on Loop One and stumbled in shock back into camp, which wasn't all that unusual of an occurrence.

Moments after the race started, the noise of a huge tree crashing to the forest floor right next to the yellow gate caused consternation among the bystanders. Everyone who remained at the yellow gate and some who had already left rushed over to the side of the road to peer through the darkness at the size of it. It was a large ramrod straight tulip poplar. It had just missed crushing the runners on the road where they had been standing before the race began.

It was as if the race course itself had thrown down the gauntlet and said, "Look at me! You can't win, mere mortals! I am all-powerful!"

## Chapter 4: Danger Falls

*Loop One, clockwise, early Saturday a.m.*

Danger jogged easily in the line of runners up the switchbacks of the first mountain. There was laughter and joking amongst the competitors, and hopes were high.

The beams of their headlamps lit up the white metal tree plaques when they reached the trail at the top. Their feet barely touched the ground as they flew fearlessly over the Pillars of Doom. They raced in a strung out pack through rocky outcroppings, then down through the darkness of the Deep Woods. They crashed through the dead branches of the pines, automatically protecting their eyes with their arms.

At the book location, he joined the jumble of people anxiously waiting to tear out their book pages. There were people frantically screaming, "Hurry!" at the person at the book. Danger knew that Book 1 was always a bad few moments of race time. Once he ripped out his page, he chased other runners along the old road, tore through the clutches of the briars, and clambered over the side of the road onto the dreaded Jaque Mate Hill.

## Danger Beyond The Yellow Gate

There were fresh foot slide-out places everywhere from the runners ahead of him. The slope was steep and slick, especially in running shoes. Tangles of saw briars and giant roots had to be beaten through and traversed. There were yells and curses as runners slipped and fell. The lights from all of the runners' headlamps were shining up and down the mountain, as if someone had strewn a bucketful of stars across the hillside.

He used both of his hiking poles to his advantage on this section. Using two poles with two legs (2 X 2) was similar to using 4-wheel drive, he thought. It gave him more power, and that was important for the ultimate in speed and quickness. He was doing well, maneuvering around obstacles with no major problems. He was beginning to feel cocky and decided to speed up.

Suddenly, in the middle of the descent around a cliff, he started sliding through the rocks a little too quickly. One of his feet became tangled up in a pile of rocks and down he went on his butt and back, clutching his hiking poles. It happened so fast that there was no way to stop the fall. His head fell back and smashed into a rock, and his headlamp and knit hat popped off his head and flew away into the darkness. His mouth opened in pain, and he inadvertently let out an anguished scream, and then the world spun away into blackness.

A stream of water splashing on his forehead and cheeks awakened him. Opening his eyes, he saw someone standing in the spotlight formed by his headlamp. The light was shining up from the ground right below where he had landed. The person was standing on the flat rock by his head urinating on him! But then, on second glance, he saw that the person was actually emptying the contents of a plastic water bottle onto his head. Danger could see two blue-jeaned legs, which didn't seem right somehow.

Danger rolled over onto his side, held his head, and groaned. "Oh no," he muttered. He looked at his watch and saw with relief that only a few minutes had passed. Lifting his head and peering down the slope, he saw someone running away into the distance. Then he sat up and gingerly touched the back of his wet head, moaning, and seeing stars. His hand came away bloody. What a sorry way to start the race! He was mad at himself for falling.

A group of runners came avalanching down beside the cliff, and one of them hesitated mid-stride upon seeing Danger lying there. "You okay, Danger?"

"Yeah, no problem," said Danger, stubborn as ever.

"Is this how you got your name?" The runner asked, attempting to make a joke about Danger's predicament.

"Nah," said Danger, automatically adding: "Safety is my middle name."

The runner said, "Now that's a paradox," and kept going.

"Jerk," mumbled Danger under his breath.

For a few minutes he remained dazed and disoriented. He put his old red bandana over the wound on the back of his head and put some pressure on it to stop the bleeding. The pain subsided some, and he rounded up his headlamp, poles, and hat, then continued descending the hill, cautiously and groggily. His back hurt miserably, and his legs felt stiff.

He hadn't even once thought of giving up. But he had lost the main pack of runners and had fallen behind on time. Now he would have to play catch-up if he wanted to stay in the race. He shook off his worries and pain, and got his head back into the race as best he could, realizing it was going to be a long few hours until the sun came up.

# Chapter 5: Duct Tape

*Loop One, clockwise, early Saturday a.m.*

Frozen Ed was up at the Book 3 location, ripping out his book page. A group of four followers surrounded him and were anxiously watching his every move. Ed had been coming to the race for many years and was a veteran of the course. Many virgins, as first-time runners of the race were called, had successfully made it around Loop One by attaching themselves to Ed like cockleburs on a pair of old boot laces. Everyone knew that he knew the way, so it was easy to follow him and let him navigate.

Ed was in his seventies now, and one of the oldest persons to ever attempt the race. This morning, he was wearing brightly colored yellow and orange tights, so he was easy to spot in the group.

Danger wondered if Frozen Ed minded being with a group of virgins. Ed was a gregarious man, always laughing and telling stories. He seemed to enjoy having a group of followers, and he liked to show off his course knowledge by narrating the interesting parts of the course as he led his entourage around. But Ed had also told Danger that he liked being alone out in the woods. So he probably had mixed feelings about being in a group.

Sometimes Ed played jokes on his merry band of followers and pretended to go east when he should have gone west, or vice versa, just to see if they knew the way. Upon occasion, one of the followers had used their beginner's luck to steer Ed in the right direction, so having a pack of wolf cubs follow you around was not all that bad.

Sometimes if Ed got to a book location first, he would grab his page and take off, scraping the newbies. This tended to cause a panicked reaction among his followers.

Today was no different than any other race day. Frozen Ed joyfully took off down the other side of the mountain after getting his page. The rest of the group scrambled to get their pages, and the last one carelessly slung the book away as he left. The group's main fear at that moment was losing track of Ed, whose navigational skill was their hope of surviving the first loop.

Danger arrived just as the last one took off. The book had been thrown into the saw briar patch, so he retrieved it and tore out his page and tucked it away in the plastic bag in his shirt pocket. He put the book back in its plastic bag in the hiding hole and even took the time to cover it with the heavy rock. laz and RawDog had outdone themselves in choosing enormous rocks this year.

It would be so easy to follow Frozen Ed and not have to navigate the route himself. He was surprised he didn't have his own little clutch of parasites, because they generally attached themselves to veterans like him. But he guessed the fall and the time he had lost on Jaque Mate Hill had prevented that from happening.

His head hurt and a lump was forming on the back of his skull. He reached around with his hand and tenderly palpated it with his fingers. It was covered with a patch of dried up blood, and he pulled his hand away quickly and left it alone. It seemed to be healing on its own accord.

Danger wondered who the man in blue jeans had been who had poured the water in his face to wake him up. Someone had actually spent a few moments of their precious race time to give him assistance. He was grateful. But it was strange. Nobody wore blue jeans in this race. It was tights, or lightweight hiking pants, or shorts. Blue jeans would protect you from briar cuts, but they would weigh your legs down, and especially drag you down if it rained. And if the person wasn't in the race, then Danger would be disqualified for receiving aid from someone outside the race. But if you were unconscious and received assistance without your consent, did that count? These were all questions he would ponder and find out the answers to at a later time.

The full moon was shining down on the summit, and he noticed large, flat rocks and a mature forest. He didn't have time to admire the place, though. The watch controlled his life, and he checked it and jotted down his split time in a little notepad he kept in his shirt pocket. Immediately over the summit lay the rest of the north section. He kept his head down and plunged down the slope, headed for Son of a Bitch (SOB) Ditch. It was steep down to the Boundary trail, which laz called a "Candyass Trail" because it was maintained.

Someone was limping back on the Boundary Trail towards him. He was unhappily shaking his head back and forth when he got close to Danger.

"I'm done. I'm going back to Quitter's Road while I've got a chance. This is so bad! Look at my leg!" the fellow said in anguish. His face was contorted in misery and pain.

Race number one was on his bib, which meant he

had been named the Human Sacrifice in the race. He was living up to his name.

Danger looked down, and his headlamp showed a dark strip of cloth tied around the injured runner's calf. His tights had been torn away from the wound and used as a bandage. There were streams of blood oozing out from beneath the piece of cloth. He must have fallen or run into a sharp stick.

"You should put some pressure on it for a few minutes to get the bleeding to stop. Then cover it with a bandage and slap some duct tape on it and keep going," advised Danger.

"Oh no, no, my race is over. This is terrible!" cried out the young man, shaking his head in dismay.

The young man totally ignored Danger's advice about putting pressure on the wound and limped away. Quitter's Road was an old jeep road that led to the campground, so he didn't have far to go. The injured runner should be there within an hour or so, depending on how fast he hobbled, and a bystander would probably drive him to the emergency room, if he wanted to go. He would probably be the first runner to quit.

Danger thought about how sometimes runners gave up after injuries like this, but sometimes they just

## Danger Beyond The Yellow Gate

kept going. It all depended on their pain tolerance. There was no first aid assistance out on the course, and there were no medical personnel in camp. If you got hurt, you had to depend on your own resources. Danger thought that he could have managed with some alcohol wipes and duct tape. After all, duct tape fixed just about anything.

He continued on to the enormous SOB ditch, which had to be twelve feet across and eight feet deep. Runoff from waterfalls above and water rushing down the mountain after rainstorms had caused the ditch to erode deeply into the mountainside. There were several choices for crossing it. He could take the easy little maintained trail at the bottom that simply dipped through the ditch. There was no one around, so no one would see that he was off course. Or he could slide down through the dirt into the pit of the ditch, then grab the tree root that stuck out and snaked up the side, and pull himself back up the other side. This was the most difficult way through it. Or he could slide down through the dirt into the pit of the ditch, then walk a few steps up through the bottom to an easier way up the other side.

He chose the hardest way possible: down to the bottom, then pulling up by the root. His reasoning was that he had come to do the world's hardest race course, which was always the most difficult way, so why would he take the easy way out? It didn't matter that there was no one there to see whether he had stayed on the route. He would know that he had cheated if he chose the easy way through, and that would have haunted him forever.

## Chapter 6: The Meeting at the Cairn

*Loop One, clockwise, early Saturday a.m.*

The fog at the coal ponds caused him a brief moment of panic. He was sorely tempted to pull out his compass to find his way through. The fog was like swirling smoke, and he was surprised by trees suddenly rising up like sentinels in pockets of light about him. The compass was in his pocket, and he knew how to use it. He had even set a bearing earlier, just in case. It was good to have it with him so he was prepared for any eventuality. But he stubbornly plunged into the chilly fog and made it through without ever pulling the compass out of his pocket.

He climbed the steep switchbacks through the rising mist and achieved the top easily. The audible click in his ankle that sounded with every step as he climbed annoyed him terribly. An old injury from too much abuse hiking the Appalachian Trail had left him scarred for life with a permanent click.

Book 4 was ahead. He jogged up the hill on the jeep road and heard the low hum of voices, interspersed with sudden outbursts of laughter. It must be runners at the book. He sped up, eager to greet old friends and hear a few stories from the race thus far.

But instead of runners, he saw a strange scene ahead in the misty gray, early morning light. There were two old men huddled together, shoulders hunched, looking down at the ground. The smaller one was pointing at the dirt with a long stick and drawing something. As Danger got closer, he could hear him saying, "This is the river, and this is the peak above it. If you go this way, you will fall to certain death." He was drawing a map in the dirt and trying to explain it to the other guy.

The bigger one replied, "Does it have lots of 'runner-friendly' laurel at the top? *Heh heh heh!*" He had a cruel tone to his voice, and Danger couldn't tell if he was joking around or serious.

As he approached, they looked up, and then stood up straighter, watching him as he made his way to them. His first thoughts were, "What the heck are they doing out here? Must be illegal spectators. But how did they get here?" It was miles of hiking to come in from the State Park side, and miles of four-wheel driving from the other side.

As he drew up next to them, he said, trying to sound official, "You know spectators aren't allowed out here, right?" Because he put out the books and the water drop, and usually blew the bugle, he did feel some ownership towards the race.

## Danger Beyond The Yellow Gate

They gazed at him solemnly. The bigger one had wild eyes that didn't seem to focus anywhere and equally wild hair that was in a froth of silver and gold curls around the sides of his balding head. His long beard was the same color as the hair on his head, but curled down his chest. His belly hung over the belt on his old blue jeans, and his jacket was unbuttoned. Hat in hand, he answered with a grin, "No, we're not spectators. We're out here looking for an escaped con, name of Clyde. Have you seen him?"

Danger was taken aback. Escaped con? Why didn't they have on uniforms and guns? "Noooooooooo….." he said, nervously. "Haven't seen anybody except runners." He had heard nothing about an escaped con from anybody else. What was going on here?

The shorter man stood there quietly, his mouth in a grim line, with a thick gray mustache parading down both sides to his chin. He looked fit and ready to take off into the woods after the escapee at any moment. He carried no extra weight, wore dark green pants and jacket, and seemed more serious and stern than the bigger one. But then he broke into a grin which made Danger think twice about his true nature. "He'll be along eventually. We always catch our man."

"Are you prison guards?" asked Danger, curiously.

The bigger, bearded one spoke up. "Nah, used to be. Now we only chase Clyde. He escapes all the time. Loves to run, that Clyde. Comes out here and runs the race course when he escapes. Loves it out here. He never wants to leave the race course."

The fit looking, shorter fellow politely said, "I'm Harry, Lieutenant Harry Stockstill, and this here is Lieutenant John Rankin."

"But shouldn't you be hurrying to catch him?" asked Danger.

"Nah, he'll turn up. We're not worried," said John, the taller, bearded one, shrugging his shoulders. He seemed very nonchalant for a prison guard chasing an escaped con.

The early morning light was causing the fog to recede down the hillsides, and visibility was slowly improving. Danger was becoming increasingly anxious about the race. He looked at his cheap wrist watch and said, "I've got to get going. Is the race still on?"

Harry said, "Yeah, sure, we don't ever stop it."

"Yeah, unlike my dang chainsaw. That stupid thing stops all the time," interjected John, shaking his head back and forth.

"John, I told you to get the stabilizer and use it every time. Then it will start and keep going all day," said Harry impatiently.

"It's too damn high-strung for me," said John.

"Good grief, just get the stabilizer like I told you a hun-ert times," said a frustrated Harry.

John bitched about his chainsaw for a minute more, and Danger kept looking at his watch. Finally, he started walking to Kerry's Cairn, and the two old guys tagged along. The fog had dissipated in the morning light, and he noticed that the trees on the hillside were blackened at the bases as if there had been a fire in the area, but the leaves were beginning to sprout out in the canopy, and the groundcover beneath them was greening up with spring. The forest was beautiful in the slanting rays of early spring light.

"We need to say hello to Kerry," said Harry.

"You knew him?" Danger said, surprised.

"Yeah, sure. He's a good guy," said Harry.

John looked at Harry from over the top of his eyeglasses and mouthed, "Was, was a good guy."

"Yeah, Kerry WAS a good guy," said Harry quickly.

Danger merely shook his head, wondering how they knew Kerry, the one that the cairn had been built for. Maybe they were into politics, like Kerry had been. It was common knowledge that Kerry had fought for the race to be allowed to continue in the park, and it wouldn't be held today except for his efforts. When he died suddenly, runners had started building him a cairn at one of his favorite spots on the race route. Now every runner dropped a rock on top of the cairn to build it higher. The cairn had soon become the "Memorial Cairn" for all those past runners who had since passed away.

He heard a high-pitched yipping and thought maybe it was dogs; then his second thought was wild turkeys. But he peered quickly over the crest of the ridge and thought he saw a small pond below in the last clinging rays of mist, really just a wet spot, with frogs splashing into the murky water. Spring peepers were up early calling for mates.

Danger found the book marking his spot on the course and tore out his numbered page from it. Then he carefully replaced the book in the baggie and returned it to the hole, and covered it with the large rock laying nearby. He didn't want to make it any easier for the next runner than it had been for him. Every runner should have to move that giant rock. He carefully put the new book page with the others that were in the plastic bag he kept safely in his buttoned inside shirt pocket, and then he prepared to walk on down the hill.

The two old men were still standing there, looking down at the book's hiding spot, and discussing the title of the book: *How to Make Good Choices*. The title of the book went with the self-help theme of the library of books marking the course this year.

"You think you have a choice, but you don't," said John, appearing to be in a thoughtful mood.

"Sure you do; you have free will," said Harry.

"No, you're wrong. You're an idiot," said John, pretending to curl his lip as if he was about to snarl.

"No, you're the idiot. Everyone knows it," retorted Harry, laughing to himself while making short, quiet snorting noises through his nose.

Danger got the feeling that these two could go on and on about any subject all day long and never get tired of each other's company. He tried to slink away while they kept bantering, but John said, "Come here and look at this cairn." Danger had no choice but to obey.

The cairn was about three feet tall, made of bigger rocks at the bottom and smaller ones at the top. There were chunks of dark black coal interspersed throughout. One of the rocks was different than the others and had the curved ridges of a large fossil embedded in it.

"Stu's rock," said John, quietly pointing it out to Harry.

"Yep," said Harry.

Harry turned to look at Danger and said, "Don't you need to put a rock on Kerry's Cairn?"

Danger said, "Oh, yeah, I forgot," and bent down to find a flat lichen-covered rock. As he placed it on top of the cairn, John and Harry did likewise with their own rocks. They smiled and seemed satisfied to have added three rocks to the pile, and stood there admiring their work.

"Kerry will like that," said Harry.

John looked at Harry sternly over the tops of his bug-eyed glasses again.

"Kerry WOULD have liked that," stammered Harry quickly.

## Danger Beyond The Yellow Gate

"I've really got to get moving," said Danger. He was catching up after his fall, and wondering again if this year would be his year to finish the Fun Run. He was not sure about five loops, or even four, but he thought the Fun Run was in his grasp if he could get away from these two old farts and get back to the race. A nap in camp would be helpful, and some real food, maybe some chicken when he got back to the campground. But it depended on who was cooking the chicken. If laz was cooking the chicken, it was bound to be bloody and raw with a burned outer crust. Surely the official Chicken Cook, scRitch, would be there, and his chicken was always cooked through perfectly and not dripping blood. He longed for a piece right then for breakfast. But he still had miles to go before he could get back to camp, and it was no use dreaming of chicken.

He started trotting away, lifting his hand in farewell, and the two old guys looked up and hollered, "BYE!"

"See you later, Danger," added John.

"Good bye!" said Danger, figuring and hoping he would never see them again.

Danger turned to the task at hand, taking long strides to move quickly away, but swiveled his head to look back once. He saw the gray, bulging cairn in the early morning light, but the two old geezers were gone. He guessed they could move faster than he thought they could.

## Chapter 7: Losers at the Buttslide

*Loop One, clockwise, early Saturday a.m.*

Danger dropped down the muddy little hill to the water drop and filled up his reservoir from one of the cluster of water jugs set out on the ridge. Some of the jugs were already empty and had been thrown carelessly down the hill. There were two jugs, half empty, that had been carried partway back up the hill by some runner in a hurry to get going.

Suddenly, the wind came up over the ridgeline roaring like a freight train bearing down on him. He yanked his lightweight wind breaker loose from the side loop on his pack and threw it on to keep from getting cold as the chilly wind attacked him from behind.

Maybe he would see the two Lieutenants, Harry and John, again farther along the course. Possibly they would catch Clyde by then, though. But maybe they were hallucinations, merely tricks his mind was playing on him. They had seemed so real! If only he could get back to camp with enough time left over from this loop so he could take a short nap. That would surely help to clear his head so he could think.

He pondered over the meeting with the two old fellows. Who were they and how had they gotten on the course? How had they known Kerry? How did they know his name? Why weren't they in any particular hurry to find the escaped convict? Where were the trackers with guns and dogs? He didn't have any answers, but thought there was more to it than met the eye. He would ask about them back at camp. Since cell phones were not allowed on the course, it was impossible to find out anything now.

It was a relief to be free and running again. So much of the route was steep and unrunnable, but the old jeep roads were where time could be made up. The solitude of the place enveloped him. As he loped along, he stuffed his thin jacket back into a pack loop, chewed on a chocolate protein bar and imagined it was chicken, and sipped cold water from the spout of his hydration pack. Breakfast at last. He had on loose, lightweight hiking pants with plenty of pockets for snacks so he could eat on the move. His pack was small but had outer straps for holding things he put on and took off as the temperature changed throughout the day and night. His map was folded in his shirt pocket, but he rarely pulled it out. The compass was also in that pocket. His book pages were tucked away in the interior buttoned pocket of his shirt because they were precious and could not be lost. The pants and long-sleeved shirt, in addition to thin leather work gloves, prevented most of the briars from ripping him to shreds, but his face and neck were raked in places and raw from the thorns he had already battled on parts of the course. The race showed no mercy even to the super prepared. He had been there so many times before, but it was still a difficult challenge that always tested his grit.

After another off-trail jaunt, he ran into two other runners at Bobcat Rock at the top of the Buttslide. They were sitting dejectedly on two large rocks by the side of the road, munching on some snacks, with their shoulders hunched over, and looking miserable.

"What's going on, Frank?" he asked the one he knew.

"Hey, Danger. The Buttslide almost killed me. I thought Mark was going to leave me to die," said Frank. His cap was on his head backwards, with tufts of auburn hair sticking out the front, and his red and black striped tights were slashed in places up and down his legs. His running shoes were muddy and wet, and Danger could see his calves were covered in cuts from the briars.

"Yeah, it was fun to watch him suffer," kidded Mark, the dark-haired runner that Danger had never met before, but took an instant dislike to for some strange reason.

"We went out too fast at the start of the race and burned up. We can't keep up the pace. Everyone took off and left us. I'm ready to head on back to the campground, but Mark here wants to stay out a while and keep looking for book pages so we'll know the way the next time we get in the race," explained an exhausted and unhappy Frank.

"Nice rat bites," said Danger, pointing to Frank's calves. "I think that's pointless, getting the rest of the pages. I mean, who cares if you do that? And what makes you think you'll get entered in the race again?" He knew the chances were slim that the Race Director would pick anyone's name two years in a row, now that the race had become so popular.

"Well, we might," said Mark, thrusting out his chin with renewed determination in his dark eyes. "We've worked hard to get this far, and we want to prove that we can find our way around and get to all the books. Then at least we can hold our heads high when *Taps* are played."

Whenever a runner called it quits, *Taps* was played

on a bugle at the yellow gate. Some runners found this humiliating because, after all, *Taps* was played at funerals. Some found it so embarrassing that they tried to avoid it by sneaking back into their campsite and not going up to the yellow gate. When that happened, laz and the bugler (most likely Danger) would go and find them and play *Taps* outside their tent. But some runners considered it an honor to be "tapped out" if they did their best in the race, and stood ramrod straight with their hats off and their hands over their hearts while the sad refrain was played for their demise in the race.

Danger had seen all kinds of runners endure being tapped out. He thought Frank and Mark were going to be of the humiliated variety.

"That's dumb," said Danger. "If you're not going to try to finish a loop, you ought to just go on back to camp. They'll be wondering about where you are." He remembered the search team he had been on a few years back looking for a runner lost on the first loop, and how the runner had spent the night in the woods and then caught a ride back into camp. The anxiety in camp had been pretty high.

"Thought about quitting a while back, but kept going. Mark here is pretty stubborn!" said Frank, exasperated.

"I just hate DNF-ing when I put so much training into this thing. At least if we get most of the book pages, that will be something," said Mark, his mouth in a grim line.

"Well, do what you want. But I think it's stupid," said Danger, tightening the straps on his pack.

"Whatever, I don't care what you think!" said Mark, tired of trying to make a point.

"OK then, I'm going down the Buttslide. Have a good time," retorted Danger, opening his eyes wide, sighing, and shrugging his shoulders. He just didn't understand some people's foolish philosophy.

"See ya, Danger, Good luck out there," said Frank.

"Hey, have you all seen anybody strange out here on the course?" Danger suddenly remembered to ask about the prison guards he had encountered earlier up at the cairn.

"No, only runners," said Frank, looking puzzled.

Danger didn't bother to explain, but started down the steep slope, concentrating on his foot placement so he wouldn't fall again. His back and head still hurt from his fall earlier.

Those two runners at the top were losers already,

but determined to make a show of it by finding the rest of the books. He didn't give a rat's ass what they did. All that mattered was to keep on going. He was determined to finish Loop One. After that, he would see about Loops Two and Three. Loops Four and Five weren't even in his sights.

The ground beneath him shifted and shook as he raced down the steep rocky slope. Stones rolled away from his feet, and he strove to keep his balance by flailing his arms to his sides as he slid through the dirt. If he stayed light-footed all the way, he might keep from falling. But if he lost his footing, he would lurch and tumble down the slope along with the loose rocks. It was a great mental effort to totally concentrate and stay upright with the gravitational pull, as well as an athletic endeavor.

When he finally made it to the book, and then turned to ascend straight back up, he had black thoughts of shaking the Race Director against a tree so the back of his head rattled against the trunk and his mouth slung saliva while he whined. Going down and back up that hill on every loop was like digging a deep hole and filling it back up, and then digging it up again, over and over. Actually, the whole race was like that. Every loop was a torturous repeat of misery.

He stayed in the black mood all the way to the top, and then shook it off. After all, it was his choice to run this race. And he really loved the puzzle of putting the course together both mentally and physically.

After college, he had hiked the Appalachian Trail from Georgia to Maine by himself. He had used his college nick-name, Danger, for his trail name, and it had stuck after that. Now everyone called him Danger instead of his real name. He wasn't quite as much of a risk-taker as he had been when he was younger, but his wife still got upset for some reason when he used their rickety old ladder to climb up onto the forty foot high roof of their house.

It seemed a natural progression to run the world's hardest race after hiking all those Appalachian Trail miles, so he did. The race course was his home territory. Although he had DNF'd every time he had run it, it wasn't because he didn't know the way, but because he couldn't do it in the time limit. A guy had to be super human to do that. He had a lot of respect for the runners who had finished the race.

This year he still wasn't in as good a shape as he needed to be in to succeed. He had almost given up on running the race again after he hit thirty years of age, but had surprised himself by deciding to try it again this year. He actually thought he was doing better than usual because his navigation had been near perfect so far. Except for the little fall on Jaque Mate Hill, he thought he was doing pretty good so far on his fifth try at the hardest race in the world.

# Chapter 8: The Chase up the Middle Finger

*Loop One, clockwise, Saturday a.m.*

Danger continued on the course, enjoying climbing up through laz's Rebirth Canal in Bobcat Rock, and sitting on the old truck bench for a moment at the Pool and Spa. He called this the Massage Chair, because after all, it was a pool and spa. The bench faced the mountains in the distance, with its back to the pond. Had the truck bench been brought to that remote location by a vehicle or by people carrying it? He also wondered if there were any fish in the little pond, and was it a good fishing hole, and knew he would never find out.

He noticed a dead tree nearby completely stripped of bark. The innards of the tree were shredded and pieces were lying all around it on the ground. It looked like a giant scratching post for a cat. The damage had been done too far up the tree for it to have been used by a bobcat. Maybe a bear or a mountain lion had used it to sharpen its front claws while standing on its hind legs. A shiver of fear involuntarily ran up his spine.

After a moment's rest, he was off again, making a stop at the Borehole in the rock to collect another book page, and traversing the jeep road and the boundary to the river crossing and the highway. There were quick, friendly greetings as he passed several runners through this area.

The highway crossing had a few media people standing about next to their cars, taking videos and pictures of him as he ran across into the woods on the other side, but he mostly ignored them. There were too many of them for his liking these days, as the event had gotten too famous for its britches. Getting his picture made annoyed him, so he scowled at them all while they shot footage for whatever documentary or newspaper article they were working on. They rarely interviewed him in camp because he was so good at looking mean.

Down through the woods, over the little rivulet on slippery, mossy rocks, and straight up the Middle Finger Ridge. Easy to find, and easy enough to climb after all the other steeper hills he had finished. And the woods here were pleasant, with birds calling in the trees, and a friendly breeze blowing on his face and evaporating the sweat. Perhaps Middle Finger Ridge was in between Fore Finger Ridge and Ring Finger Ridge, but he didn't think that was the real reason it had been so named.

Suddenly he heard voices ahead, and he could

barely make out the words of someone explaining, of all things, how to remove a tick.

"You have to find the pointy tweezers, you know, the kind you have to buy from a scientific supply company. But that's what you need to grab onto the back of the head of the tick. Then you pull very gently and very patiently, until the tick starts to let go of your skin. When that happens, you can pull the tick the rest of the way out and rub alcohol on the bite. Make sure you look at the tick under a magnifying glass so you can be sure you got all of the head out. Finally, you light the tick on fire and burn it up, or you smash it with a rock."

He recognized Harry's voice, and saw him sitting on a downed tree up ahead, facing downhill. Who was he talking to?

He kept climbing, and heard John talking. "My method is to yank the tick out in one swift jerk. If the head gets left in, it will fester and work itself out like a splinter does." He saw John leaning his back against a huge red oak tree, with his feet standing in the flat place on the upslope root anchor of the tree. His legs were slightly spread apart, his upper torso was bent over his hiking stick, and he was looking up innocently at Harry.

## Danger Beyond The Yellow Gate

"Oh, you do not. You're just messing with me. If you don't get all of the head and mouthparts out, you might get Lyme disease or rocky mountain spotted fever," said Harry vehemently.

"But if it already bit you, the bacteria are already in you, so it really doesn't matter if you pull the head out right away," argued John.

They both saw him then, and said, "Hey, Danger."

"Hey, Harry, John. Did you catch that escaped con yet?"

"No, he's too fast. And we're too old and slow," said John.

"Speak for yourself," said Harry.

John grinned, and said, "Harry's in pretty good shape, but me, I got old too fast. These legs have blocked arteries, and they hurt all the time, and I have to stop and rest so the blood flow from my heart can get all the way around and through my legs and back to my heart. Hurts like heck."

"He whines and moans about it all the time, too," said Harry. "I give him an A for effort, but an A- for all the whining. Then he brags when he makes it to the top of a hill, so he gets an A--."

Danger kept pushing up the hill past them, hoping they'd understand that he had to stay focused on the race. They started following him, and Danger topped out on a small rise in a mountain-laurel hell. He either had to push through the thick bushes or follow indistinct animal paths through the maze of branches.

There was a sudden noisy rustling in the laurel bushes to his left, and out of the corner of his eye he saw a flash of blue rushing up the hill. "*Whaaa*?" he sputtered in surprise.

"It's Clyde!" hollered Harry. "Get him!"

Danger didn't even think twice about it, but took off into the laurel hell and beat his way through, with every limb scraping his throat and legs like hands reaching out and trying to grab him. Clyde ran ahead, long brown hair whipping in his face, blue work shirt, and blue-jeaned legs with feet encased in old work boots pumping up the hill just beyond. Danger slung off his pack and hiking poles to lighten his load, and leaped after him. Clyde was fast and seemed to practically fly uphill. Danger was fast too, and when he was almost on him, he threw himself at Clyde's feet like a goalie after an incoming soccer ball. He thought for sure he had him, but he landed with a thud, and his hands

## Danger Beyond The Yellow Gate

wrapped around a small tree trunk instead of Clyde's ankles.

His face had slid through the duff on the forest floor, and he had to spit out tiny rocks and dead leaves. Standing up, he wiped his hands on his pants and his mouth on his shirt sleeve, and peered uphill. Nothing but trees. No sign of Clyde anywhere.

Harry and John were right behind him, and he retreated back past them to fetch his pack and poles. Slinging his pack over his shoulder, he said, "I thought I had him. I was sure I had him! But he got away. Sorry, guys."

"That's okay, happens all the time. He's one slithery snake, isn't he?" said John.

"We can't chase him like that anymore. It hurts too much. You gave it a good shot," said Harry.

"So how do you plan to catch him, then?" Danger asked, exasperated.

"Why, it's not that hard. We wait for him at the tops of hard climbs when he's all tuckered out and can't catch his breath," said John. "Then we just gang up on him and grab him. Easy."

"We always get our man," reiterated Harry.

John looked at his watch and said, "Don't you think you better get moving? It's getting kinda late. I'm thinking you need to be back to the yellow gate before 1605."

"1605?" said Danger, puzzled.

Harry sighed, rolled his eyes, and explained, "He's using military time. John likes to confuse people. Just keep adding numbers from 12 noon instead of starting the count over at 1 pm."

"Oh, 4:05 p.m.," said Danger. His watch was set to race time, but he easily made the conversions in his head. "That's right. I need to get over to Meth Lab Hill. I'd better hustle."

He started to take off, but Harry hollered at him, "Hey, don't forget your book page!"

Danger had to backtrack into the laurel to get his page, cursing under his breath. Harry had saved him from screwing up royally.

Harry was saying to John, "You know, that stump tree has 'character.'"

"Nah, it used to have character when it was a living tree. Now it's just a stump," countered John. "Doesn't have much weight to pull it down in a storm anymore, so that's why it's still standing."

## Danger Beyond The Yellow Gate

"It's still a cool stump. Look at all those black patches on it that look like faces," argued Harry.

Danger waved good bye to Harry and John, who seemed like old friends of his now. They were still arguing about the stump tree and struggling through the mess of the laurel hell.

Meanwhile, Danger was back on course, studying his watch and re-evaluating how long it would take him to get to Rat Jaw. His left knee hurt from the dive after Clyde, but he flexed it and decided it would be okay after a while if he just kept going.

He wondered if he could catch up with Clyde, and what he would do if he did. Maybe Clyde was dangerous? He might have a gun or a knife and come after him as revenge for trying to catch him. Well, he didn't have a choice. He had to keep going on the race route or quit. It was do or die time.

## Chapter 9: Big Hell

*Loop One, clockwise, Saturday afternoon*

Danger felt like he had been climbing repeatedly up and over all the wrinkles in an old Indian's weather beaten face, pockmarked with warts and craters here and there. He was stuck in an eternity of climbing, where everything on his body hurt from the constant friction with the ground and from his fall earlier.

Now he was climbing up the horrible mountainside nicknamed Big Hell. It seemed to go on forever into the blue sky. His calves and quads were worn out and screaming for rest, and his left Achilles felt stressed to the max. His heart was beating wildly into overdrive in his chest, and his breathing was ragged. If only he could take a rest somewhere, but he looked at his watch and knew that it was impossible.

He came upon Harry and John resting with their backs leaning against the uphill sides of two trees. Waving at them, he said, "No time to talk, guys."

Somehow they had gotten ahead of him. It seemed like they knew the course as well as he did.

His Dad had taught him how to navigate on their many trips into the woods. He had instructed, "If

## Danger Beyond The Yellow Gate

you know where you are, then you can set a bearing to your destination. But if you don't know, you first have to orient the map using landmarks you can see, and make an educated guess about where you are. Sometimes you have to give up for the time being and backtrack to where you last knew where you were."

But Danger rarely used the map while in the race. He had the course memorized from being out there so many times, and he had pored over the map at home to refer to places he had been. During the event, he kept the clock and his location on the course in the forefront of his mind. The map was always in his head, and he was moving through its landscape. He could see himself running through it, the contour lines falling behind him, watersheds entered and exited, streamlines approached and crossed. This interior gift of navigation was like the birds knowing exactly where to go when they migrated south to Central America in the winter. It was something he took totally for granted and used to his advantage.

The relentless climb was almost over. When he reached the top, he bent over, hands on knees, and regulated his breathing. Then he stood up, squared his shoulders, and gazed off into the distance through his cool blue, metallic shades. He saw the mountains on the horizon covered up by big white clouds rolling in. There were shadows playing hide and seek on the hillsides, with light and dark places interspersed. He thought rain might be in the forecast for tomorrow. He continued on to the well-maintained "Candyass Trail" back to camp, thinking to himself, "I've got this! Piece of cake!"

# Chapter 10: Quick Turnaround

*Loop One finished, Saturday afternoon, in the campground*

The run down from the last book had been easy, and he made excellent time to the yellow gate. laz took his book pages and counted them and asked if he was ready for *Taps* to be played. Usually Danger was the one who played the bugle, but he couldn't very well tap himself out, so a replacement had been found. But Danger shook his head no and hurried down to his campsite to get ready for Loop Two. His Mom was there, and she hugged him. His Dad patted him on the shoulder. Bibi was helping Bob heat up soup for him, not just any old soup, but homemade chicken noodle soup made by Danger's wife, Bella.

"Heard anything from my girls?" he asked.

"Bella called. They're both fine. She said they would come out sometime, maybe tomorrow," said Bob.

"Good," Danger said, smiling happily.

Danger sat in his lawn chair and pulled off his filthy shoes and socks, checked his feet for blisters, popped one, stuck on a bandage and a piece of duct tape, and put on the dry socks and shoes that Bob had set out for him. He showed his Mom the lump and scab on the back of his head, and she cleaned it up some, and taped a bandage on it.

Meanwhile, the soup was hot, and he started in on a bowl of it. Lots of noodles and chunks of chicken. Bibi handed him a blueberry muffin, and he wolfed it down. Next, a banana, closely followed by a bowl of mashed potatoes. He was eating as fast as he could and trying to rest a little, too. There was no time for a nap, though, as he only had twenty minutes to get back to the yellow gate. It was still daylight, but soon evening would come and chilly temperatures, and then it would be nighttime on the counterclockwise loop. He made sure he had extra batteries for his headlamp.

Bob said, "Sposed to rain in the morning. I'm sticking your rain jacket in your pack. Got your cap and polyester gloves?"

"Yeah," said Danger. He hated wearing rain gear of any kind. "But gloves are for girls," he added.

People started cheering loudly, as someone was seen running up to the yellow gate. His Mom and Dad and Bibi hurried away to check on who it was and find out the news.

## Danger Beyond The Yellow Gate

"Listen, Bob," said Danger in a conspiratorial tone after the rest of the family left. "I don't want anybody to think I've lost it, but I've been seeing these strange people on the course. Two old men out looking for an escaped convict from the prison. But they don't have guns or dogs, and they are never in a hurry. And I've seen the con they are chasing too, and he's always on the course. It's all really weird. Have you heard anything from anybody about an escaped convict being on the loose?"

"Noooooo," said Bob, a puzzled look on his face.

A couple of runners who had DNF'd stopped by the campsite to shake Danger's hand and asked Bob if he needed any help. Bob told them everything was fine, and they meandered away.

"You might be having hallucinations," said Bob. "You fell and hit your head. Maybe that's what started it."

"Yeah, I was wondering about that," said Danger.

"Maybe if you could get some sleep, they would go away," said Bob.

"No time, no time," said Danger, shoveling in more food. "Don't tell Bella or Mom, okay?" he said, not wanting to worry them.

"I won't. But I might talk to Dad about it," said Bob.

"OK, but I'm still going out on Loop Two," insisted Danger.

"Did you run into Frozen Ed?" asked Bob.

"Yeah, passed him at the road junction. He was with Mike and Alec. Looks like he's feeling pretty good."

"Yeah. He might make two loops this year," said Bob. "Sam and Phil left a couple of hours ago."

Danger nodded his head. His path had crossed theirs on Big Hell.

"Three of the Frenchmen are still out there, and several others," said Bob.

Bibi returned and excitedly said, "It was Amanda and Emily finishing Loop One! They're planning to eat something and get back out there."

Danger thought he was as ready to go as he would ever be, so he stood up, pulled on his pack, and trotted to the gate, shaking the stiffness out of his legs.

## Danger Beyond The Yellow Gate

Bob rushed after him, handing him his forgotten hiking poles. scRitch hurried over and handed him a quarter of freshly cooked chicken, wrapped in a paper plate and paper towels. Danger's eyes brightened and he quickly stuck the package of chicken in the top of his pack for later. He got his new race bib number, touched the yellow gate, and started down the road through the camp, with everyone cheering and waving.

"Loop Two, Loop Two!" repeated in his head like a battle cry. He had surprised himself, making it to the second loop, and he was exultant.

# Loop Two Begins

# Chapter 11: Curs and Curses

*Loop Two, counterclockwise, Saturday evening*

He practically flew down Big Hell, making good time so far on Loop Two. The fact that it was a counterclockwise loop did not faze him at all. He hit the correct spot at the bottom with dead reckoning. Angry barking echoing through the holler stopped him before he could bag the book page from its hidden location.

Three dogs of various sizes were running along the trail across the creek. They saw him and began howling. They zeroed in on him and plunged into the water. There was nowhere for him to go but back up Big Hell or across the creek at the fork. They started zipping in at his heels and trying to bite him, coming in low and fast. He danced in circles and used his hiking poles to try to push them away, but the poles weren't strong enough. He lashed out with his feet, kicking them in their slobbering mouths, but that didn't deter them either. They followed him as he splashed across the confluence.

"Damn it! Get lost! Bad dogs!" he yelled, but they

still kept after him.

He bent down midstride and grabbed some rocks out of the stream and pitched them at his tormenters, striking them in the heads and flanks. The dogs seemed to get even more vicious at this.

One of them was a medium-sized white cur with short legs but maddening speed. It rushed in, snapped at his ankles, took a beating from his hiking poles, whipped around, and rushed in from another direction. That one seemed to be the main attacker, but the other two hounds followed, dashing in when the first dog gave them an opportunity.

Danger was high-stepping backwards along the side of the tributary, trying to keep all three in his field of view and fend them off. A rock tripped him up, and in an instant he was flat on his back on the ground. The white monster was on him, aiming to get at his throat and rip it out. Danger was madly fending him off with his hands.

Suddenly, one of the dogs behind yipped loudly, and the monster dog's ears pricked up. He slid over Danger's chest and took off running with his tail between his legs. The other two followed closely behind, and they all splashed across the creek back to the trail from whence they came. Danger lay there, panting, wondering how he had been freed so easily from his tormenters.

Just then, John and Harry came striding up. "You okay, Danger?" called out a concerned Harry.

"Yeah, just some nips, not too bad," said Danger, taking stock of his wounds. "They came out of nowhere!" He lay there a minute more, catching his breath.

"Damn local curs. People around here leave them running loose. They are usually pretty friendly. Guess you seemed like a threat," said John.

"What made them take off like that? Were they scared of you two?" asked Danger, getting up from the ground and bending over the stream to splash some water on the cuts on his ankles and hands. There wasn't much bleeding, as the animal's teeth had mostly scraped off the top layer of skin.

"I don't think we're all that scary," said Harry. "Do you?"

"Must have heard their master calling. Probably supper time," mused John.

Danger was suddenly very tired. In fact, he felt downright exhausted. "I just need to rest for a

## Danger Beyond The Yellow Gate

minute," he said, finding a rock to sit on by the creek. The water rushed noisily over the mossy rocks, oblivious to his problems.

John sat on a rock next to him and companionably looked at the water, too. After a few minutes, he said, "Why do people do this race anyway?"

Danger rubbed the back of his neck and said, "I don't know. I guess you do it to see if you can."

"There's the constant stress of the time limit, finding your way in the woods, the fatigue, the dark, the weather, and you have to be aware of what you're doing at all times," said John. "There's no time at all for cruising or resting. Why would anyone want to deal with all that?"

"And the crazy local dogs are a real bonus, too," added Harry, standing off to the side.

John suddenly asked Danger if he was married.

"Yes, I sure am. Coming up on three years," said Danger.

John said in a serious tone, "This might not apply to you, but I always tell people who are thinking about getting married to strap a badger to your leg for a week." Then he said the next part with a huge grin, "It will be about the same as getting married, except that eventually the badger will let you pet it."

Harry rolled his eyes and sighed loudly. "He always tells that story. Thinks he's so funny."

John was in a silly story-telling mood, and said, "If you saw a hot beer propped up in the hollow of a tree, would you drink it?"

Danger replied, "Heck, yeah."

John said, "We did that. We put a beer in the hollow of a tree by a book location. We watched it. But no one drank it because of the bad best buy date!"

Harry rolled his eyes some more.

Danger reluctantly pulled himself away from the distraction of the silly conversation and stood up, adjusting his pack. "Listen, I've got to get moving. I'll probably see you later," said Danger. He hopped across the rocks of the small tributary. As he started up the short trail to the Zipline, John called out one last silly remark.

"Okay, sounds like a 'wiener' to me," said John, smiling and waving good bye.

Danger had only gone about 30 feet when he heard Harry calling his name urgently.

## Danger Beyond The Yellow Gate

"Danger! Did you get your book page?"

"Well, crap. No, I did not," sighed Danger. He stomped down the trail and back over the creek to get the page and stuffed it angrily in the bag of pages in his pocket. Harry and John were watching and nodding.

Once again Harry had saved the day. He owed him big time.

# Chapter 12: Befuddled on the Bad Thing

*Loop Two, counterclockwise, Saturday night*

Danger wasn't too surprised when he got to the top of the ridge to the Eye of the Needle and found Harry and John sitting there on large rocks, proudly looking like they owned the mountain. He didn't know how they did it, but they had gotten ahead of him again. They seemed so old and slow, and John seemed to always be in pain, but there they were.

He said in an exasperated tone, "How did you two get here before me? It's just not possible unless you sprouted wings and flew up here."

Harry looked him in the eye and said, quite seriously, "You should know that the impossible is possible out here."

John added, grinning, "Yeah, and we have our shortcuts."

Suddenly, a deep and frightening roaring rose up from the hills in the distance. Danger held his breath and his hackles rose. "What was that?" he asked.

John answered in Spanish, stroking his beard, "Ella es una perra loca."

Harry translated: "She is a crazy she-bitch. A

panther." Then he added, "Her name is "La *Norrraaahhh!*"" He gutturally growled the last part of her name.

"I heard on the news that the panthers might be returning to this part of the county," said Danger. "But couldn't it be a bobcat?"

Harry confidently answered, "No, the bobcat sounds more like a woman screaming. Catamount sounds throatier."

Danger's eyebrows knitted together at the catamount word.

John explained, "There are many names for a panther: painter, cougar, puma, catamount, mountain lion, big cat, she-bitch. This one has been living here for many years. Her territory is the rocky outcroppings and ridges all around us on these mountain tops. She has a *baaaaad* temper. Look out for her. You don't want her to see you running away."

Harry spoke up then with his knowledge about mountain lions. "If you see a cougar, it's because it's stalking you, intending to eat you. They usually hunt during the evening or nighttime, and jump on their prey from behind. It is said that sometimes you can scare one away if you fight back. If you run away, you are triggering its attack mode."

"Is she the only one around here?" asked Danger.

"She had kittens several years back, but they all took off to carve out their own territory. The father left too, but sometimes comes back. Wants to visit the missus, I guess," said John.

"I hope I don't run into her. But I've got to get to the prison," sighed Danger, and started walking that way.

Harry and John stood up like old men stiffly getting out of bed first thing in the morning. They started walking with him down the steep hill called The Bad Thing towards the old abandoned maximum security prison in the valley.

"The runners have made this into a veritable trail," said Harry.

"What does that mean?" asked Danger.

"Real good. It's a real good trail," answered John.

"Nah, that's not right," said Harry. "Crude. It's a crude trail," he said.

Danger suddenly belched, and John said, laughing, "Was that satisfying?"

## Danger Beyond The Yellow Gate

This launched John into a story. He told them about the time when he ate too much spicy Mexican food and had sudden bowel movements and was running off the trail into the bushes by the side of the river.

"Not only sudden, but toxic," said Harry. "There were reports of a fish kill in the New River."

John's shoulders rose and fell as he laughed at Harry's joke.

Danger started speeding ahead of them, and he heard John change the subject behind him, whining, "I don't know how it can be so easy going down when it is so hard coming up this thing."

"It's called gravity," muttered Harry.

"What's that? What'd you say?" asked John.

"Nothing. Nothing at all," said Harry.

# Chapter 13: Rat Jaw Apparition

*Loop Two, counterclockwise, Saturday night*

It was merely another steep climb, but not really. There was nothing in the race quite like Rat Jaw. The ridiculous climb under the powerline was almost vertical in some places, and he had to bend over to use his hands like a four-legged creature to keep his balance. His leather gloves were useful in all the briar tunnels, but the wiry saw briar branches still attacked him, neck and cheek, wrapping around his head like long tentacles attaching to his back. He ripped his way through, and the razor cuts stung like fire. Six-inch stobs where the briars had been cut back tripped him up and slashed into his ankles at every other step. The short briars were the worst, because they wrapped around his ankles and tore mercilessly through older cuts.

His hiking poles were of little use, so he stowed them on the side of his pack for the climb. For part of the climb he was able to use a downed powerline like a climbing rope to pull himself up. Finally, he made it to the crack in the cliff and climbed up. Not much farther to the road. The full moon was intermittently shining down through the dark clouds that had been accumulating all evening. Up ahead, he thought he saw the black shape of someone

## Danger Beyond The Yellow Gate

moving up the last pitch to the road.

Maybe he could speed up a little and catch them. He hadn't seen anyone in a long time. There might be spectators at the road as well, with news of other runners.

But when he crested the hill at the road, there was no one about. No spectators anywhere. He guessed they were all asleep back at camp. There was no sign of the other runner either.

He ran up the road to the Observation Platform, but there was no one there either. The water jugs were sitting deserted on an old wooden table with crooked legs next to two picnic tables. He grabbed a jug and sat down to pour water into the reservoir of his pack. A candy bar was stuffed into his mouth and the book page ripped out. It would be nice to take a nap on the table, but glancing at his watch, he saw he had no time to dally.

Loading up his pack, he started back down the road to run down Rat Jaw the same way he had come up. Directly below him, his headlamp spotlighted a runner wearing blue jeans. It must be the escaped convict, Clyde.

"Clyde!" he hollered.

But Clyde, if that was indeed who it was, ignored him and tore down the hill like a dog afraid of gunshots.

The moon was passing behind the ominous black clouds again, and the moonlight was waning. Danger switched his legs into overdrive, and flew down the hill after the dark figure below.

He slid down the crack in the little cliff and fairly plummeted down the slope that he had so recently struggled up on all fours. His feet attacked the hillside and his legs flexed and pinioned him to the ground over and over so he did not fall.

The moon came back out momentarily, and he peered down the slope hoping to catch sight of the person, but there was no shadow racing ahead. He had lost him.

But he had gained valuable time with that wild descent, and he had found new life in his legs. He kept the speed up as he continued on down the rocky creek to Book 8. Maybe it was the sugar rush from the candy bar he had just eaten, or maybe it was the thrill of the chase after the escaped con, but he suddenly felt great.

He realized that if he kept going, he was going to have good times and bad. Sometimes the bad times seemed overwhelming, but if he pushed ahead he would eventually come to a good stretch. Kind of like real life, he thought.

# Chapter 14: Nice Kitty

*Loop Two, counterclockwise, Saturday night midnight*

By the time he had navigated to the Pool and Spa in the dark, the sugar rush from the candy bar had terminated. He was left feeling weak and drowsy. Maybe he needed to eat something more substantial. He sat down on the old truck bench and looked out at the mountains and the sky. Very little could be seen as the rain clouds had nearly filled in the sky now, and the moon sometimes peeked out like an eye winking. Opening the top of his pack, he found the chicken quarter sitting there, covered with greasy paper towels. His pack smelled like barbecued chicken now, but he didn't mind; he liked the smell. Hungrily, he tore pieces of perfectly cooked dark meat from the bones and savored every bite, then washed them down with gulps of water. The chicken was delicious, and the fat and protein calories would pump up his muscles for more running, he thought.

When his belly was full, and all that was left was gristle and bone, he threw the remains over his shoulder into the pond and wiped his greasy fingers on the already saturated paper towels. He stuffed them and the paper plate into the top of his pack,

## Danger Beyond The Yellow Gate

yawned, and decided to lay down on the bench for a minute or two. He tucked his feet up on the bench and put his pack under his head.

As soon as his body was horizontal, he was instantly asleep.

Dreams of bright light entered his mind, and his wife's beautiful face was next to his, whispering softly in his ear.

"Danger, Danger," she cooed.

"Bella, my Bella," he breathed.

"Danger, wake up!" she whispered insistently to him as she moved away.

"Come back, Bella!" he moaned.

"Danger, wake up!" he heard again, and this time a pebble hit him squarely on the nose.

He opened his eyes, but did not see Bella. Someone was whispering to him from the trees close to the bench. He turned his head and looked that way and saw a man in blue jeans hiding behind a tree, holding up his finger to his lips. It must be Clyde, the escaped con.

"*Shhhh*, don't say anything. Don't move a muscle!"

said Clyde in an urgent whisper, pointing toward the pond.

Danger was alarmed, but he couldn't resist the temptation to slowly lift his head up and look over the back of the bench toward the pond.

The moon was shining down on a huge cat lapping water at the edge of the pond. Its muscles rippled down its back and flowed into powerful legs. The long tail was tipped in darkness. The mountain lion had not seen him. Yet.

After it finished drinking, it started scuffling at something in the water at the edge of the pond, and Danger realized it was trying to get the bones he had thrown into the water. The panther reached its massive head down to its paw and started crunching away at the captured bones.

Danger could hardly breathe, and he was afraid he might cough with the stress of the moment. His eyes were about to pop out of his skull with the alarm he was feeling, and his hair was standing on end on his arms and the back of his neck. He started shivering uncontrollably.

The catamount finished its appetizer and licked its whiskers.

## Danger Beyond The Yellow Gate

Danger shifted his weight slightly, and his pack suddenly slid off the bench.

The noise caused the cougar to flip around and position itself into attack mode, haunches up, head low, tail flipping back and forth.

Danger jerked his head down out of view and slithered onto the ground below the bench in a heap of jelly-like muscles. What should he do? He couldn't think of anything except to lie there and play dead. Oh my God. The mountain lion was coming for him. The tender faces of his wife and little girl sprang unbidden before him, and he covered his eyes with his hands to try to hold that vision closer.

The giant she-bitch was almost upon him. She leaped onto the back of the bench and looked down at her victim, roaring madly into the night.

Danger knew he was a goner. There was no hope. He prayed for help.

Suddenly, the panther gave an angry "*meowrrrrrrrr*," and leaped off the bench back towards the pond. She loped away, but turned once and screamed up at the sky. Then she disappeared into the forest.

Danger was still lying on the ground, quaking in his running shoes, waiting for the claws to rip him open and the mouth to tear into his belly.

But there was no attack. The cat was gone.

He pulled back his hands from his eyes and lifted his head tentatively. There were two feet right next to his head, and blue-jeaned legs rose up into the last gleam of moonlight.

"I told you not to move!" chastised Clyde. "She almost had you for dinner! She roams these ridgetops from dark to dawn looking for prey. You just got lucky. Best not to sleep out here."

"Why didn't she attack me?" asked Danger, sitting up shakily.

"La *Norrraaahhh* doesn't like me worse than she doesn't like humans," answered Clyde, emphasizing the end of the cougar's name with a low growl.

"And that chicken was a bad idea. Keep your eyes open for her; she might still be close by," Clyde said as he moved away down the hill.

"Wait!" Danger cried out. But Clyde had taken off.

Danger was left alone and puzzled. Why was the cougar afraid of Clyde? Nothing made sense.

## Danger Beyond The Yellow Gate

Grabbing his pack and hiking poles, he started galloping crazily down the hill towards Bobcat Rock. All he felt was fear, and he couldn't breathe. His head jerked left and right as he looked for the she-bitch to come out of the darkness after him. Where had Clyde gone? Why had he left him all alone with the mountain lion still about?

Oblivious to the briar-infested path, he tore through the sharp prongs as if they weren't even there. The pain would catch up with him later when the adrenaline wore off.

Clyde and the mountain lion had both vanished into the night. Danger had to stop for a moment to catch his breath. The fatigue and fear were messing with his mind. He reminded himself that when you panic, you make bad decisions. He had to stop and sort things out.

Bobcat Rock was bound to be a terrifying place. It had always seemed like the perfect haunt for a cougar. But he had to combat his fear and go through laz's Rebirth Canal to stay on course.

He just had to.

# Chapter 15: French Bread

*Loop Two, counterclockwise, very early Sunday a.m.*

The moon and stars were being covered up by banks of swollen white and gray clouds moving across the sky at a stately pace. Danger felt like rain was coming, but maybe not for a little while.

As he pushed himself up and over the mountaintop and retrieved his book page, his headlamp spotlighted two people sitting on one of the huge couch-like rocks beneath the summit. They were in the midst of a discussion. He realized he had come upon Lieutenants John and Harry again, and he greeted them eagerly.

John was telling Harry about his trip to France and his love/hate relationship with the French bread he ate there every day.

"You have to try it, but not if your teeth are loose like mine were at the time. I didn't get new teeth until after that trip. They eat French bread with everything. You just have to tear a piece off. They sop up every drop on their plates with it. They have to get the crust cooked just right. It's kind of like the consistency of your shoe."

## Danger Beyond The Yellow Gate

Harry asked, "Is the inside eatable?"

"Oh yeah, all of it is delicious. I was ashamed not to eat the crust, because everyone else does. It was good. I'd eat it with a bunch of meals, but then I had to take a day off because it was hurting my mouth."

John continued, "All the houses there were at least a hun-ert years old. The Grandmother cooked all day. You would have liked to have her at your house!" John was smiling happily at the memory. "The first week I was back home, everything I ate was a disappointment."

Danger was standing in front of them, pivoting one of his hiking poles back and forth from its wristband, and anxiously trying to interrupt. He wanted to tell them about the mountain lion. He was feeling hungry, too, and broke out a ham sandwich.

"So what's up, Danger? How's it going out there?" finally asked Harry, turning away from John to acknowledge his presence.

Danger told them in between mouthfuls of sandwich all about his run-in with the mountain lion. He asked, "Why did she run away from Clyde?"

John slowly answered. "The two of them have a

long relationship. Clyde has stalked her throughout her habitat for years. Cats have more than the regular five senses, so she feels his presence differently than you do. She's afraid of his aura. She thinks he is a 'haint.'"

Danger was surprised by that word, and asked, "A 'haint'?"

Harry explained. "Old timey word for a haunt. She thinks Clyde is a ghost."

"Well, is he?" Danger asked, swallowing a big lump of sandwich.

"Not quite," said John.

Before Danger could ask more questions, a runner suddenly appeared, rushing over the knob after finding the book. It was still dark, but Danger realized it was Amanda when her high-pitched voice called out, "Hey, Danger! What are you doing standing around? Better get a move on!"

"Hey Amanda, how's it going?" asked Danger.

"Emily has been having diarrhea, but otherwise we're doing pretty well," said Amanda.

Emily caught up just in time to hear the news about her diarrhea, and said with embarrassment in her

## Danger Beyond The Yellow Gate

voice, "You didn't have to tell Danger about that!"

"Oh, well, if you wouldn't have eaten all those dates and raisins, look where we'd be now," scolded Amanda.

"You ate them too. It's not my fault that your stomach is made of iron and mine isn't!" Emily said angrily.

Danger wisely kept his mouth shut, wondering to himself why these two females were running together when all they did was fuss and fume at each other. Neither one of them seemed to notice John and Harry sitting on the rocks.

"That ginormous rock over the book is so heavy," Amanda confided as she and Emily passed by, beginning to speed down the hill, Amanda in the lead.

"Oh, it is not, you're just a wimp," said Emily.

They melded into the darkness, and Harry said, "See, even girls can do this race."

John laughed and disagreed, saying, "No, it's statistically impossible. Girls are ten percent slower than men across the board for all kinds of races. A girl will never be able to finish this race unless she is a female Sam."

"Or a female Logan," said Harry. "But it could happen."

"I would love to see that," said John.

Danger started making his move to leave, and they followed him. He thought he beat them down to the trail, but John's face suddenly leered at him from behind a tree at the bottom. "Beat ya," he jeered.

How did he do that? Sometimes John was painfully slow, but sometimes he was able to put on a burst of speed, especially racing downhill.

"See you later, Danger," said Harry, as Danger sped away.

"Are you going down to Book 2?" called out Danger, as he turned around and looked back.

"Yeah, we always do that part. But we hate Jaque Mate Hill. He made me go down it once, and I cursed him the whole way. So we use a shortcut," said Harry.

"When are you going to catch Clyde?" asked Danger.

"Soon enough," said John, waving good bye.

# Chapter 16: The Deep Woods

*Loop Two, counterclockwise, Sunday predawn hours*

The air had a moist, clingy feel to it, and Danger knew rain was imminent. Then the rain began. At first it was like the patters of little cat feet on the moss around him, and drops of water tickled his face. He bent to open his pack and find his rain jacket, cap and polyester gloves. Right before the shower hit, he was ready for it. Or he thought he was.

The rain started coming down in curtains of darkness, and the wind whipped around his body. His thin jacket caught and shredded on the sharp pine branches, allowing the cold rain to pour through and soak him anyway.

Stupid rain jackets never worked. Soon he was completely drenched by the icy rain, and the shivering began. The water continuously dripped down the back of his neck. He knew that he would soon be back in camp where warm food and a hot shower would make everything alright again.

The mossy floor of the forest was littered in pine needles and pine cones. Puddles of water formed where divots of moss had been pawed over by the local boar population. The wallows made by the boars were sunken things of mud now, and he avoided them as best he could.

Thoughts of goblins and mountain lions consumed him. The darkness of the pre-dawn hours and the sudden drenching rain put his mind on dark and evil creatures of the night. They could be hiding behind the trees or up in the rock outcroppings ahead, ready to pounce upon him.

A huge poplar tree loomed before him, with the area at its base covered with dead oak and poplar leaves, thick and soggy, and toilet-paper-like in consistency. He sunk into them and kept climbing. His feet were soaked through and sliding around in his running shoes. His toes were cold and numb, but splashing through puddles seemed to warm them up.

There were some interesting rock formations in the outcroppings where he imagined small mammals sitting and eating nuts, as evidenced by the nutshells strewn about. But the goblins and mountain lions must have eaten all of them and not even left the bones.

Coming over the top of the rocky grade was another

wet and miserable form. Danger met the other runner as he continued upward through the rocks. They were two dark shadows in the night, conversing loudly over the pouring rain.

"How you doing, Danger?" shouted Amanda.

Danger grimaced. "Okay I guess. Are you on Loop Three?" he yelled back, knowing the answer.

"Yep! I hope this crap stops before Jaque Mate Hill!" she replied. He saw that she was shivering and hopping back and forth from one foot to the other as she talked with him, trying to maintain some core warmth. Finally, she stopped and stood still with the rain dripping off the brim of her cap.

"Yeah, it sucks," said Danger.

"You coming back out to play some more?" asked Amanda. Her eyes seemed to be glazing over in his headlamp glow.

"I don't know yet. Depends on my time when I get to camp," said Danger, shrugging his shoulders. He looked up the hill and saw another headlamp weaving its way towards them, probably Emily trying to catch up.

"Well, get a move on. You can do it!" she encouraged him, shaking off her sleepiness.

"You too. Go for it!" he replied. "But look out for the mountain lion! She's prowling about."

"Oh no, really?" she said, fearfully, and hesitating. "I thought that was all stories made up by Iaz."

"No, she's out there, and she's pissed off."

Amanda pursed her lips and frowned, and said, "Well, I am too, so she had better look out!" Her righteous anger propelled her forward into the rain, and she began to leave. Just then Emily caught up, but did not get a chance to even catch her breath, as Amanda took off.

Emily practically squealed, "Damn it! Wait up!" Her voice sounded tired and frustrated. She kept running after Amanda.

Danger continued climbing up the mountain. He looked back once and saw Amanda's tiny form descending into the pit of darkness with Emily's tall, slender figure following right behind.

# Chapter 17: Back in Camp

*Loop Two finished, early Sunday a.m. in the campground*

Danger finished Loop Two with a little buffer of time. He rushed down to the shower house to get warmed up under the hot water. Bob followed close behind, bringing him hot soup and fresh clothing.

"Any news from my girls?" asked Danger from the shower. He stood in the hot water relishing the fact that it was not the cold rain. The soup cup was on the bench next to him, and he picked it up and ate while he showered.

"They're coming out today. All's well at home. Bella said tell you she loves you," said Bob, still hanging around by the sinks. "Did you get any sleep on this loop?"

"Maybe a few minutes at the Pool and Spa before La *Norrraaahhh* almost ate me."

"La *Norrraaahhh*?" asked Bob, quizzically.

"Yeah, the mountain lion."

"What? You got attacked?"

"Yeah, sort of, but Clyde scared her away."

Bob didn't know who Clyde was, so Danger told him all about it.

"But don't tell Bella or Mom, okay?" pleaded Danger.

"That all sounds crazy," said Bob.

"I know. I'm going back out on Loop Three, though. Nothing can stop me. How is everyone else doing?"

"Sam and Phil are out there on Loop Three," answered Bob.

Danger had seen them speeding along.

"Maybe you'll see them later today. Amanda and Emily recently started on Loop Three. There's still several others out there on Loop Two. Then there's two people out there on Loop One who still haven't found their way back."

"Frank and Mark, I bet?"

"Yeah!" said Bob.

"They're trying to get all their pages, even though they have quit," explained Danger.

"That makes no sense," said Bob.

## Danger Beyond The Yellow Gate

They walked back up to the campsite quickly. Fortunately, the rain had stopped, so they didn't have to huddle under the tarp. Danger ate two grilled cheese sandwiches, applesauce, a banana, and some of Bella's homemade peanut butter cookies, and washed it all down with a diet lemon lime soda.

He was exhausted. His mind and body craved sleep, but always there was the clock before his face, urging him on. He was slouched in the lawn chair, head in his hands, when his Mom came over, took one anxious look at him, and said, "Just look at you! You shouldn't go back out there!"

That made him get up and grab pack three and his hiking poles and head to the yellow gate. Nobody told him what to do. Especially not here, when he had come so far. Loop Three loomed before him.

# Loop Three Begins

# Chapter 18: Back to the Deep Woods

*Loop Three, clockwise, Sunday dawn*

"Uno, dos, tres, quatro…," Danger was having fun counting off the switchbacks up the first mountain in Spanish. His stomach was full of all the calories he had consumed, so he was moving slower than usual. The storm had come and gone, but the trees were still dripping all around him. The trail was a rushing rivulet of water in some places, filled with rain water flowing down the mountain. The early morning light was peeking through the tree branches, and it was going to be a beautiful day. The gnats had come out in swarms after the rain, and if he stopped for even a moment, they flew into his eyes and mouth—another good reason to keep pressing onwards.

The view from the gap showed mountains of a lovely slate blue on the horizon. He could see the ridge that came up from the other side of the campground. His path lay to the left up to Arrowhead Rock.

The huge arrowhead-shaped, upended slab of stone looked like a doorway opened up to another world.

## Danger Beyond The Yellow Gate

John and Harry were standing by it, waiting for him.

"Hey," said Danger.

"Hey back," said John.

"Thought we'd walk with you for a spell," said Harry.

"Sure," said Danger, agreeably.

The three of them walked single file beyond the big rock and past scenic vistas from rocky outcroppings. Danger gazed out at the watershed below and could see the Deep Woods to the left and the deep cuts of strip mine benches across from it.

A little farther, and he looked up into a rock house with an overhang high up on a cliff face. Piles of dirt had been dug out and washed down a crack in the rock.

John saw him looking, and said, "That's where La *Norrraaahhh* lives. She patrols at night from here to the other side of the park along the ridge lines, hunting for prey, and comes here to sleep in the daytime."

"You mean she might be in there now?"

"Maybe. Want to go check?" John said with a gleam in his eye.

"No thanks," said Danger, looking anxiously up at the cougar's cave.

They came to a place where the path ended in a cleft of open air and started back up on the other side. Luckily, there were pillars of stone sticking up in the opening, so crossing was similar to rock hopping across a stream.

But it wasn't so easy for John. The pillars were very slick after the rain, and his old boots were smooth and slippery on the bottoms. At first, he decided to crawl across on his hands and knees. He made it out to the first pillar this way, and sat down on his butt to assess the situation. He lifted himself up on his hands and scooted his butt over to the next pillar, then did the same to the next one. At the edge, he put his feet down on a rock, and pulled himself up and over the rim, rolling onto his back.

"Not a pretty sight," said Harry.

"Yeah, but I made it," said John.

Danger had almost laughed out loud, but checked himself.

The trio continued walking, then veered to the top

## Danger Beyond The Yellow Gate

of a little rise in the hardwood forest. They crossed an old road cut and went on down through the sandstone rocky outcrops and some loose boulders.

They were moving through the boulders when John said, "I meander at a glacial pace uphill until I finally get there, but I can walk pretty fast downhill." He looked down and said, "Look at that. Nice fossil."

They hurried across a flat, messy looking ridgetop that had branches blown down from the storm and passed under a huge uprooted tree leaning against the top of another tree.

"Widow-maker," said John.

"Thought it was a black tupelo," said Danger, using the name he called all trees when he didn't know their proper names.

"No, it's a black cherry, but the hillbillies call it black churry," corrected Harry. "And actually, it's not technically a widow-maker. A partially chain sawed tree with dead branches that fall off and kill the chain saw-er below is what is really called a widow-maker," he added.

"*Huh,*" was all John could come up with in retort.

Finally, they were in the pine forest. Harry

explained how the coal miners had strip mined up to that elevation and planted white pines.

"Funny how the pines grew in these straight rows," said John, jokingly.

There was the dead thunk as they broke through the lower pine branches, breaking pieces off easily. The forest floor was littered with branches, cones, and soft pine needles. The sunlight was filtering down through the pine canopy. Danger could see the blue sky and the drop-offs to the right and left of the ridge they were walking on. He looked up the trunk of a pine and saw the branches were all whorled around the center trunk in evenly spaced rows. The point they were walking on was getting narrower. Above the canopy, the wind could be heard rushing by, leftover from the storm, but down below, it was barely felt.

John pointed out a pile of red dirt beneath the end of a downed rotting tree. "Some animal clawing for grubs," he said.

They came to an old road bed. "An old haul road," said Harry, "used to be used for hauling coal."

They slid down the hill to Book 1's location, and Danger got his page. They pulled themselves back up the little hill by holding onto tree trunks.

## Danger Beyond The Yellow Gate

Danger hurried on down the old road, pushing through the briars and avoiding the muddy hog wallows. Harry and John followed at a slightly slower pace, and he could hear John wheezing.

The ridgeline could be seen in the distance, and it was washed out light blue against the bright blue sky. John and Harry caught up to him as he gazed at the horizon. Harry said he knew every peak's name, and started listing them off.

Danger continued on and reached the place to drop down Jaque Mate Hill. John and Harry were right behind him. Harry bent down and pulled up a long blue zip tie sticking out from the moss. "This yours?" he asked Danger.

"No way," said Danger.

"Good. We hate cheaters," he said, pocketing the zip tie.

"Look out there, Danger," said John. "Can you see the confluence from here?" he joked, pointing off into the distance.

"Sure, it's just right there," said Harry, grinning.

Danger said, "You all are nuts," and started descending down the hill through the enormous twisting vines and prickly underbrush.

"Once you start down that thing, you can't quit," said John. "Because if you quit, you just have to climb back up it."

Danger paused, listening to the world beyond. He could hear the wind roaring back up through the gap at the top of the mountain. "I won't come back up it," he promised.

John said, "Don't you use a compass? One time we got here and the compass was not pointing in the right direction. I wanted to go down the mountain anyway. We would have been lost for two days. It took 30 minutes to look at the map and think. Harry was a rock. He had his compass bearing, and he was not going to budge. It took 20 minutes to convince me. That was the one and only time I got him to go down there."

"I don't need no stinking compass," scoffed Danger.

The fall down the cliff on Loop One was forefront in his mind, and he planned to tread very carefully this time. The plan was to hit the little tributary that merged with the big creek where he needed to go. The creek had probably risen from all the rain, and it might be rushing down the mountain full of brown chocolate milk water by now. But that would be a ways down there, over the slick cliffs and through the torturous drops. He dreaded the steep climbs and descents of Hiram's Vertical Smile and Apple Cow Lips that lay beyond.

Harry and John wouldn't follow Danger down Jaque Mate Hill, like two old horses refusing to leave the barn, so the three of them separated. Danger fully expected to see them again.

# Chapter 19: The Math Question

*Loop Three, clockwise, Sunday morning*

Danger slowly made his way up to Book 3. His feet and legs were trashed. It would be so amazingly easy to quit here and walk back on Quitter's Road, and he was toying with that idea like a cat pawing at a captured mouse.

The enormous flat stone couches looked inviting, and he sat down on one to go over his split times out loud. Harry and John came down from the summit behind Danger and sat on either side of him.

"Hey," said Danger, happy to see them again.

"What are all those numbers you're blabbering about?" asked John.

"My split times. I try to keep the same amount of time between points on every loop, but this loop is killing me."

There were clumps of moss scuffed up all over the rock they were sitting on. Danger had a vision of a big cat pawing up the moss to make a nice place to lie in the sun. At least it was broad daylight right now, so there was probably nothing to fear.

"So do you like math?" asked John.

## Danger Beyond The Yellow Gate

"Pretty much. I made all A's in it in school anyway," Danger answered. "But the only math I feel like doing right now is figuring out how I'm doing in the race," added Danger.

"I've got a question for you. It's a question that's been debated for hundreds of years, ever since Plato lived," said John, mysteriously.

"Oh, so we're going to talk about that one now?" muttered Harry under his breath.

"Well, what is it?" asked Danger, curiously.

"Do you think that math is an invention or a discovery?"

The neurons in Danger's brain tried to attach to the question, but sputtered and fizzled, and his thoughts took a dive. He was so tired, and his legs felt like noodles. How was he supposed to know the answer to some dumb math question?

He didn't answer at first, and finally shrugged. "I don't know."

Harry was standing in front of him by now, unable to sit quietly, and his hands flew up and his mouth and eyes shot open. A snort exploded out of his nose. "What??? You mean you don't just KNOW?" He was incredulous that Danger didn't know the answer immediately.

Danger was stunned and stupefied. He was a smart young man, but this game was ridiculous right now. He was no philosopher on normal days, but especially not this day.

"I just don't even have a clue right now," he said, blonde head looking down at the ground.

Harry stomped over to the other couch rock and back several times, a mixture of disappointment and frustration on his face.

John was grinning from ear to ear. "Want me to tell you the answer?" He looked like a little kid about to burst to tell a secret.

Harry quickly said, "No, let him think about it for a while. He's got a brain of his own. If you tell him what you think right now, that will be it. He won't figure it out for himself."

"But it's obvious that the answer is 'invention,'" said John, letting out a nasty laugh. "*Heh, heh, heh.*"

"No, no, it's not. You're an idiot!" said Harry.

"No, you're the idiot!" John shot right back.

## Danger Beyond The Yellow Gate

"Stop arguing!" exploded Danger, tired and impatient.

Harry and John quieted down then. Danger's mind went round and round trying to understand the meaning of the words in the question. What exactly was an invention anyway? Something like a machine or a tool or a computer. Something people had come up with by using their brains, something to perform a particular kind of work. What about a discovery? That would be something people had found that had always been there waiting to be found. Something that people had not created.

Just then Clyde came whizzing by, not ten feet away from them. All three turned their heads and watched him ascend, not one of them making a move to go after him. John yawned, and Harry pulled off his cap and scratched at a place above his ear.

"Aren't you going to try to catch him?" demanded Danger.

"He's too fast. There's no way," answered John, shaking his head.

"I just don't understand," sighed Danger.

"You'll understand when you understand the

answer to the math question," said Harry, confusing Danger even more.

"I've got to get going," said Danger, suddenly standing up, not feeling rested at all. His stomach was upset, too.

"Ok, we'll see you later," said John.

"Try to focus on that question," said Harry, doggedly.

Danger threw his pack on and picked up his hiking poles. He took off up to the summit, glad to get away so he could be alone and think. Those two old men were getting stranger every time he met them. He could hear them still arguing as he reached the summit, and then their voices evaporated away into nothingness.

# Chapter 20: Cogitations

*Loop Three, clockwise, Sunday morning*

Danger pondered the question posed by John all the way through the far northern section. Was math an invention or a discovery? What a weird question! He tried to focus on his thoughts, but it was so hard in the midst of the dreaded Loop Three brain fog.

If math was a discovery, then it had to exist outside of people. Did it exist through all of time, waiting for people to discover it and use it to explain how the world worked? That made a lot of sense to Danger.

But maybe people invented math as time went on. It was invented to perform useful functions such as building pyramids and surveying land. People needed to invent math and money in order to buy and sell goods to each other.

Math would continue to be invented as it was needed in the progression of human civilization. But maybe not. Maybe there was already all the math possible created when the universe was created, and it was just waiting for humans to reveal it for the first time. There was no way people had discovered all of it yet. There could be an incredible amount of complex math out there that no one could ever think of to invent, but it could eventually be discovered.

Danger also thought that possibly math was both invented *and* discovered. You could think about math as being discovered by man; then man invented the language of math to be able to use this discovery and explain it to other people. So the answer could be both.

It seemed like Harry very strongly believed that math was discovered, but John thought it was invented. This seemed to be an all-consuming argument between them. If he picked invention, John would be grinning his evil grin in delight. But Harry would be so disappointed in him. He wouldn't like that.

Maybe he should let them explain their answers to him, and then he would be able to express his point of view better.

He slid down the muddy slope into the SOB Ditch, and then pulled himself up the tree root to the top on the other side. The coal ponds were bound to be foggy in the early morning.

The fog drifted by in wafts and clouds until the forest was filled with its smokiness. When he got to the coal ponds, he couldn't see at all due to the thick blanket of fog. He was so exhausted and drowsy, and he was desperately afraid he might get lost. He finally just pulled out his compass and turned the dial to the correct bearing and followed it through the fog around the coal ponds. He told himself that it wasn't defeat he was feeling, but wisdom.

At this point, he was pretty sure his race was over. Checking his split time, he saw that it was so. Even if he ran top speed the rest of the route, he was going to miss the cutoff. He had done his best, but the race course was winning.

Somewhere inside himself, he felt a certain spit of defiance rising up. He wasn't going to quit. If nothing else, he was at least going to get all his book pages. That would show them he had never quit. He remembered Frank and Mark's quest to get all their pages on Loop One, and his impatience with that idea at the time. His mind had been changed by his time out there, and now he thought he understood. The race would take away all your pride unless you fought back somehow.

The race wasn't about winning; it was about not admitting defeat. Some people carried on through the course getting all their pages even though they had DNF'd, and some returned to run it multiple times into their old age, still trying to finish it. The race was so impossible, except to a determined few who somehow defied the impossible, some of them multiple times. Danger doubted he would ever be able to finish it, but he could at least not admit defeat.

# Chapter 21: Concepts at the Cairn

*Loop Three, clockwise, Sunday morning*

As he ran up to Kerry's Cairn, he heard Harry and John having another discussion there. They were talking about Squire Knob and how it was named.

"Originally the knob was named Square Knob because the top of it looks to be squarish," said John. "But the locals had trouble pronouncing the vowels in square, and it came out *squire*. So now it is Squire Knob on all the maps, even though it has nothing to do with the name *Squire* at all."

Harry murmured, "*umm hummm*," in agreement.

John was sitting on the mossy ground, legs straight out in front of him, and Harry was standing nearby, leaning on his hiking stick. Danger sat down cross-legged next to John.

Danger was anxious to find out more of what they thought about the math question, as he had been thinking about it a lot. He decided to bring up the subject.

"You know, I have been thinking about your math question," he said to John.

John perked up and eagerly said, "And you've

decided math is an invention?"

Danger was hesitant, but decided to go on and give his opinion. "I've been thinking all through the north section. I think that God created math when he created the universe. God created the laws of nature, so then we have to discover them and find ways to express them to others. So the language of math was created or invented by us, but God was the creator of actual math." Danger felt relieved to have expressed himself, like a weight was lifted off his chest.

John was visibly upset. "No, that's not right," he said, shaking his head angrily. "The universe was created with a Big Bang, and later on people had to invent math to be able to evolve. Math is made up as we go along to suit our needs."

But Harry was delighted with Danger's answer. "So if God created math in the laws of nature, then math is a discovery. Good job, Danger."

John ignored Harry's praise of Danger and furthered his argument. "Man applies his invention to nature all the time. Just think about the perfect spiral as applied to a snail shell."

Harry began discussing his own ideas, leading Danger into deeper waters. "But there are things that exist outside of nature. There are concepts that don't need nature to exist. Such as the concept of a sphere. Even if there were no spheres in the world, the concept of a sphere still exists. Do you know what a concept is?"

"An idea?" said Danger, searching his brain for the right answer.

"Yes, an abstract idea…" began Harry.

John interrupted with his knowledge about spheres. "A sphere is a perfectly round geometric object which is completely symmetrical around its center, with all points on the surface lying the same distance from the center point."

Harry carried on as if John hadn't said anything. "A concept is something that is conceived in the mind…"

John interrupted again. "There are no true spheres in nature. The closest thing to a true sphere is the sun, but it's not completely spherical."

Danger was desperately trying to pay attention to Harry, but John kept trying to move him onto a different subject. He was about to get frustrated.

Harry ignored John and continued speaking, "So if the concept of a sphere can exist, then the possibility exists that other things outside of nature can exist, such as a Creator. The possibility exists for the supernatural, such as God, angels, devils, guardian angels."

"But what about prime numbers?" piped up John.

"No, let Harry talk," quickly responded Danger.

"He's just trying to sidetrack me," said Harry.

John got very quiet and seemed to melt into the background. He didn't give a response. He obviously didn't want to hear any more.

Harry continued, "So a concept might be an idea that is possible, like finishing this race. You can have the concept in mind and it never happens, but the concept is still real and possible. This race is a concept that changes as people have faith in it being possible and then make it possible. Once they believe that it can be done, and do the five loops, then the Race Director has to change the concept and make it more impossible."

Harry concluded, "So this race could be considered an experience with the supernatural."

John started moaning and sputtering as he clamored up from the ground. "That's a big leap there, Harry! No, this race is about people trying to show they can do the impossible by relying on their own skills and fitness. It's all about athletes trying to prove themselves."

Danger's mind was captivated by Harry's ideas. He had some pressing questions that had been formulating for some time. "So do the two of you really exist? And Clyde?"

"Of course we exist," said Harry. "But not in a natural way," he added, his mustache twitching as he grinned.

Then Danger got very quiet, thinking hard. "So the three of you have a supernatural existence?" He asked, looking up from the ground at last.

But Harry and John were already walking swiftly away towards the water drop. Danger got up to follow them and ask more questions, but they disappeared around the bend, as if they had never existed at all.

## Chapter 22: Return to the Pool and Spa

*Loop Three, clockwise, Sunday morning*

As Danger stooped and turned sideways to go up through laz's Rebirth Canal in Bobcat Rock, his breathing was fast and irregular. He was warily watching every dark space, expecting the mountain lion to leap out at him. It was early morning, but the catamount might still be hanging around. His ears were alert to any slight noise, expecting to hear her rumbling voice.

When he reached the Pool and Spa, he ran right on by, afraid she might be lurking there in the bushes. He hurried to the Borehole to retrieve his book page. As he started downhill, Harry's voice seeped into his consciousness, and he pondered their discussion some more.

He had thought that Harry was a quiet fellow until their discussion. Now Harry seemed like a teacher and Danger was his student. That was okay with him, but what a strange place to be learning about the existence of God. And now he believed that Harry and John were not even living people, but supernatural people. They seemed so real to him! They looked and talked like people, but they did strange things like appearing and disappearing at will. He had realized that something was different about them, but his focus on the race had kept him from any firm conclusions.

Maybe God had sent them to help him through the race. He knew God existed without a doubt. He didn't even need the proof that Harry offered in his lecture about concepts. His daughter Marcie was all the proof he needed. She was doing incredibly well when all the doctors had said that she might not. His prayers, his wife's prayers, their family's prayers, friends' prayers—these had all been lifted up for Marcie. God was taking care of her very well.

God was taking care of him, too. When the mountain lion was about to attack, he had prayed for help, and she had run away. He had fallen and hit his head, and been awakened by Clyde, who didn't even exist in the real world. Obviously three loops of the race were way beyond his grasp, but here he was on the third loop. Everything seemed so impossible, but it was happening anyway. He wondered if he was having a supernatural experience. Is this what he had signed up for? Or was it as John said, just an athletic event?

Someone was jogging towards him along the boundary line. It was a tall, slim, brown-haired man in shorts. It was Sam, working on Loop Four, running counterclockwise.

"Hey, Danger! How's it going?" Sam was always cheerful, even when he was exhausted.

"OK, I guess," said Danger. Sam was one of his heroes, having won the event before.

"You might just get that Fun Run this year! I know you can do it," Sam was very positive and encouraging.

"I think I am out of time, but I am still going to try," said Danger, trying to be positive.

"Never give up! You only have a few more little hills to scale!"

"Little? *Ha*!" Danger thought about the tortures of the hills ahead of him. "What happened to Phil?"

"He gave up after the Fun Run. Still, quite an effort. Listen, I'll see you at the yellow gate. Good talking with you," said Sam politely, as he continued on.

"I'll give it my best shot," said Danger. "Be careful out there."

They each went their separate ways, with miles of hills yet to summit and descend, dreaming of yellow gates and chicken legs.

# Chapter 23: Peeing on the Zipline

*Loop Three, clockwise, Sunday afternoon*

The Zipline was a treacherous slope with bad, rocky footing. The wild boars loved this hillside, and it was torn up by their snouts digging in the soft earth. There were deep wallows and turned over clumps of dirt everywhere on the descent. It wasn't a straight descent, but a diagonal one across several ridges, so he had to sidle down it, which was hard to do with any speed.

He slid through a wallow and fell on his butt, but got back up, his feet threatening to slide out from under him again. Catching his breath and looking down, he saw a swarm of tiny, early spring ticks rapidly ascending his legs. He brushed them off as fast as he could and slung handfuls of them into the weeds, looking like he was doing a wild two-step dance. He knew he didn't get them all off, but maybe most of them, if he was lucky.

Down below, he saw John standing with his back to him, shoulders hunched over, head down, in the classic posture of someone urinating. Sure enough, Danger saw him turn around, pulling up his zipper, and then he looked up and said, "Well, hey, Danger."

"Where's Harry?"

"Over there by that tree. He's lots more polite than me," said John.

Harry finished up and came out from behind the big beech tree. "John will pee just anywhere, kind of like a dog."

"Here, hold my stick a second while I hike my pants up," said John, handing his stick to Harry. "If I just had an ass, I wouldn't have this problem! But I got no 'assitol.'"

Harry said, laughing, "You've got DGS, diminished gluteal syndrome. Comes with old age."

John disagreed. "Nah, I never had an ass. I used to think that with all this running I'd have a huge ass, but my wife said there was nothing to fear. I thought I would be called 'The Assless Wonder.'"

Harry held John's stick while he hiked up his pants, and rolled his eyes secretly at Danger.

John asked, "Which one do you think is harder, Zipline or Big Hell?"

"Hmmmm. Zipline, both ways, up and down," replied Danger, thoughtfully.

## Danger Beyond The Yellow Gate

"How's that?" asked John.

"You've got all these rocks and the treacherous footing. And you've got to run down it sideways, which is hard."

"I always think Big Hell will never end, though," said Harry.

"Navigation's not too bad on either one, although descending Zipline you need to be on the correct side of the creek when you get to it, so you can cross easily and avoid the steep section on the other side. You don't even need to take a bearing if you think about where things are on the map," said John.

"Yeah, the Race Director may start thinking they're both too easy, and come up with something harder. Maybe something supernaturally hard. Then it will be perfect for you guys," said Danger.

Harry chuckled at this idea, and John just grimaced.

Below them were dark shapes moving quickly down the slope, but staying together in a herd. A group of little brown dots were weaving in and out of the herd like they were one amoeba-like being.

"Boars!" whispered Harry, pointing. "Those are the babies all bunched up. They all move together like they are one, following their moms."

They hunkered down for a minute on their heels to watch the herd of boars until they were out of sight.

"Lucky to see them. Very reclusive. They must not have smelled us or they'd be hightailing it to kingdom come," said John.

Someone was coming up the mountain just west of where the herd of boars had disappeared. The runner approached them at a fast clip. It was Amanda, on her fourth loop, looking jaunty as ever. He saw another figure way behind her, struggling to catch up. It must be Emily.

"Danger, you still got any energy?" Amanda asked.

She didn't seem to see Harry or John, although he thought they were right there behind him.

"Did you see the boars?" Danger asked her, ignoring her question.

"Noooooooo, where were they?"

"Right down there where you were," Danger pointed.

Amanda scoffed at this and said, "Nope. Didn't see that mountain lion you told me about either! I'm wondering about your stories, Danger." She pulled her cap off and ran her fingers through her curly dark hair, then put her cap back on.

"I'm not lying. You can think what you want," said Danger, grumpily. He didn't care if she believed him or not.

His stomach was growling angrily, and he was wondering what to pull out of his pack. Settling on chocolate, he pulled out one of Frozen Ed's wife's chocolate chip walnut cookies and started munching on it. It was chewy and crunchy all in one, with double chocolate chips and the walnuts added for a healthy touch. He had four more nice-sized ones in a baggie, and he looked longingly at them, but he said, "Here, do you want one?" remembering his manners.

"No thanks. I just had an energy chew. I'd better keep climbing. Give my regards to the giant twelve foot rattlesnake on Big Hell, will you?" She said this last part with a wicked smile.

Danger thought to himself that she should have been a comedian. And how could she turn down homemade chocolate chip cookies?

Amanda continued climbing up Zipline, using her two hiking poles as if they were extensions to her body. She looked strong, and Danger thought she had a good chance of being the first woman to ever finish the race. She never gave up, and he wouldn't either. Of course, she might still be passed by Emily before it was all over with.

He continued descending as he chewed his cookie, looking for the creek that should be coming up. He was more determined than ever to get his pages from Books 12 and 13, even if he finished over the time limit.

He and Emily greeted each other when their paths intersected.

"How are you, Danger?" she asked, panting and trying to catch her breath.

"Doing pretty good," he said. Danger noticed her legs were bloody and shredded, and her butt was muddy from all the slides.

Emily started whining. "Every time I catch up to her, she takes off twice as fast. I don't know why she said we'd stay together." She obviously was totally pissed off and worn out with trying to catch up to Amanda.

"But I think she is making you go a lot faster than you thought possible on this terrain," said Danger.

## Danger Beyond The Yellow Gate

Emily sighed, pushed her blonde hair out of her eyes, and reluctantly said, "Yeah, I guess so." Then she added angrily, "But I could just kill her." She began climbing the hill beyond, afraid to lose sight of Amanda.

Danger laughed to himself and kept descending the mountain.

Suddenly, he heard Harry and John right there behind him, complaining about cheaters now. Where had they gone while he talked to Amanda and Emily? Now suddenly they were back.

"I saw a gel wrapper on the trail," said Harry. "It was on a switchback cutoff. The only way you can keep those runners from cutting off the switchbacks is to put a camera on every one and watch them remotely. Make sure you tell them they are being watched, too."

"Or put a book on every switchback. That would slow them down," said John, with an evil grin.

"That would be too cruel," said Harry.

"Yeah, but otherwise you've got all these cheaters with no compunction to obey the rules," said John.

"We hate cheaters," said Harry, holding his lips in a thin line and shaking his head grimly. Danger turned around and saw Harry looking intently at him from under the brim of his black cap.

"I never cheat," said Danger, defensively.

"No, I didn't mean you!" exclaimed Harry. "Just cheaters in general."

"Okay, but I NEVER CHEAT," Danger repeated each word forcefully.

He looked like he definitely didn't want to talk anymore, so Harry and John said they were going to take a break when they got to the creek. Danger gladly took off there and left them behind.

At this point in the race, Danger was feeling pretty wasted and irritable. He had done so much elevation gain already, but there was still a mountain to climb before he could run to the yellow gate. He was sorry he had been so grumpy with Amanda and Harry, but what did they expect. He would be nice on another day.

# Chapter 24: Captured

*Loop Three, clockwise, Sunday afternoon into evening*

At the base of Big Hell, Danger looked up at the height of the mountain before him. He wrinkled his nose and blew some air out in a lengthy sigh, resigning himself to climbing it. He was tired all the way through, but he knew he must endeavor to persevere.

All the way up Big Hell, he was mocked by the birds. He knew they were Carolina Wrens by their calls of: "Cheeseburger, cheeseburger, cheeseburger!" But one of them left out one of the three notes, and was calling out a two note version, which sounded like: "Stupid! Stupid! Stupid!" over and over as Danger passed. As he made progress up the mountain, the bird seemed to flit to new trees right at his shoulder, calling out: "Stupid!" with every step he took. He looked up and around, but couldn't see it anywhere. Finally, he took to screaming, "I am not! I am not! I am not!" over and over at the invisible bird, until he got hoarse and angry. "Stupid bird!" he screamed. He realized he had reached his limits, getting pissed at a little bird.

He forgot the bird after a while in the misery of the

climb. He thought the hill was interminable. He liked that word and rolled it around on his tongue. "In-ter-min-a-ble." Five quick syllables. He turned it into a chant, saying one syllable with every footfall. "In-ter-min-a-ble." With every repetition, he picked up a foot and put it down faster. Pretty soon he was marching up the hill like a soldier on a mission. His breathing was as regular as the utterance of the syllables, too.

As he approached the crest, he saw John and Harry hiding behind the grey shadows of two oak trees. John was holding a finger up to his mouth, and Harry was pointing frantically for him to move to the left. His arm jerked in spasms and he mouthed, "Go that way!" Danger obliged and moved slightly to the left, finishing the climb.

John whispered, "Hide!" at him, so he ducked behind a tree, wondering what kind of game this was.

Harry pointed down at the ground in front of his tree, and Danger saw that a long strand of fishing line had been tied between two trees about ankle height off the ground.

Danger heard someone singing as they approached from Big Hell. He heard a silly refrain: "On top of

### Danger Beyond The Yellow Gate

lasagna, all covered with cheese, I lost my poor noodle, when somebody sneezed…"

Then he saw Clyde, head down, singing a few words with every breath, feet chugging up and down in time with the song as he finished the climb. He ran unsuspecting right into the fishing line and was tripped up as planned. He did a solid face plant into the dead leaves and dirt, hands stretched out reflexively in front to break his fall. "*Wuh*!" he said, surprised by the fall.

Quick as a panther, John leaped on top of him. It was amazing to see the old fart move so fast. He straddled Clyde's back, and held down his arms, spitting out, "Hurry up!" to Harry.

Clyde was struggling ferociously, but John wasn't budging. Harry pulled out a roll of twine from his jacket pocket, then his pocketknife out of a pants pocket. The pocketknife was kept shut with a thick rubber band. He saw Danger looking at it, and said, "It kept opening up on me in my pocket, so I had to figure out how to keep it shut."

Danger remembered something from his past. "*Hmmm*. That's strange. My old Papa used to rubber band his wallet shut."

John hollered, "Harry! What the hell are you doing?

Get over here. Now! I can't hold him much longer!"

Harry doubled up a strand of the twine and slashed through it with his open knife, cutting off about two feet. Then he bent down on one knee and grabbed one of Clyde's flailing hands. John grabbed the other one. Harry pulled them together behind Clyde's back and wrapped the twine around Clyde's two wrists three times, then tied it off. Clyde was still struggling, writhing his hips to try to get John off. But John's knees were planted in the ground and Clyde wasn't going anywhere. Harry fished a piece of rawhide out of his pants pocket and tied it to the twine on Clyde's wrists. He tied the other end to his belt, joining the two of them together for their walk down the mountain.

"Okay, let him up," he said.

John rolled off onto the ground, breathing hard. Clyde twisted to the left and right until he had his knees scrunched up under his chest, then he used his abdominal muscles to lift his upper body up so he was kneeling. Then he got one foot planted on the ground and kind of jumped up on both feet so he was suddenly standing. He abruptly started running, and pulled Harry along behind him. Harry was almost jerked off his feet.

## Danger Beyond The Yellow Gate

"Now, Clyde, we got you fair and square! Stop it!" yelled Harry.

Harry yanked hard on the rawhide, and it pulled Clyde's arms straight out behind him, which must have been painful because Clyde stopped struggling. He stopped running and looked wildly behind him, out from under his lank brown hair, and morosely said, "Well, dang it."

John pulled his own pocketknife out, pulled it open with a flourish, and bent down to slice the fishing line loose from the two trees. He wadded the line up into a ball and stuffed it in his pocket.

They all walked together along the capstones until they found some small boulders to sit on. Danger pulled out his cookie bag and generously passed it around. "Best cookies I ever ate," he said, appreciatively.

There were just enough for everyone to have one. They all munched happily on their cookies. Harry held Clyde's cookie up to his mouth so he could take big bites, since his hands were out of commission for the moment.

"What happens now?" asked Danger.

"Why, we take him to the yellow gate, of course,"

said John, shrugging his shoulders.

"Then what?" Danger pushed for more answers.

"Somehow he always manages to get loose there, and we're off again doing more loops," answered John, matter-of-factly.

"So when does it all end?" asked Danger.

"When one of us quits, or when John changes his mind about the answer to the math question. But he's too stubborn, and he won't ever quit or change his mind," said Harry. "And Clyde loves it out here, so he'll be running the race course for all eternity."

Clyde wanted to speak and quickly swallowed his bite of cookie, saying, "And Harry won't leave John, so he'll never quit either."

"I keep trying to get him to change his mind about the answer to that math question, though," said Harry.

Danger asked, "So why doesn't anybody else see you? Seems like I'm the only one who can."

"You'll see us as long as you need to. When you don't need us any more, we'll disappear," replied Harry.

## Danger Beyond The Yellow Gate

For some reason, that answer was as satisfying to Danger as the delicious cookie. Maybe he was just too tired to think much about it anymore, but it seemed entirely acceptable.

John swallowed the rest of his cookie and stood up painfully. "You'd better get a move on if you want to finish that Fun Run," he said to Danger. "Look at the sky. Soon night will be falling."

Danger looked at his watch and jumped up. "I'll never make it!" he moaned.

"Every year the Race Director seems to increase the miles, but the time stays the same for every loop," said John. "It seems impossible, doesn't it? The only way it's possible to finish is if the time expands to hold the miles. And that only happens if you have the heart to finish."

Danger listened and had to agree. The race was utterly impossible unless you had the faith and the heart to believe you could finish it. He thought of his daughter Marcie, and he thought he had enough heart for both of them.

## Chapter 25: The Yellow Gate

*Loop Three, counterclockwise, Sunday p.m.*

Danger took off running down the trail, leaving Harry, John, and Clyde behind. He waved farewell, and they all yelled good bye to him. He felt like cranking out some miles, and he knew he had to. It was a steep few miles down to the creek, and his legs were going up and down so fast that he thought he would lift off the ground.

When he was about halfway down the mountain, he was suddenly enveloped by a deep and demonic roaring. The sound came from behind him, but seemed to be all around him. La *Norrraaahhh* must be tracking him.

The rush of fear and adrenaline pushed his legs into hyper-drive, and his heart nearly pounded out of his chest. As he galloped down the trail, his head swiveled to look behind him; he was expecting her to pounce on him at every switchback. He kept repeating, "Please help me, please help me, please help me," as he flew down the rocky slope. At the stream crossing, he leapt over to the other side like a deer.

The next part was a run up a tough little ridge, but he made it to the top in record time, hearing the cougar's harsh, guttural warning once more. He ran

### Danger Beyond The Yellow Gate

down the other side through all the switchbacks in blazing speed. Was the catamount still following him? Would she recognize the boundary between road and wilderness and stay away from man's territory? He had no reason to believe she would stop at the junction with the road.

He turned off the maintained trail and pounded up the road and kept pushing himself to the campground. Did he have enough time? He didn't think so. Was she still following him? He didn't hear her any more, but she could still be there. Just a little bit farther and he would be safe.

The first person who saw him round the bend into the campground gave out the alarm, "Danger's here!"

He heard his two dogs barking madly at his campsite when they saw him coming up the road. That meant Bella and Marcie had come to the campground and were waiting for him.

Other people ran over to the road and started clapping and cheering excitedly, "Go Danger, Good job!"

He could see laz up at the yellow gate looking at his watch. He could see his family was there too. One last push and he would be there. He heard them counting down, "10, 9, 8, 7, 6, 5, 4, 3, 2, 1, 0!" and he reached out and touched the yellow gate.

"Forty hours exactly! Couldn't you have gone any faster, Danger?" asked laz.

Danger just looked at him, trying to catch his breath, and then someone pointed to a chair and he collapsed into it. Before he even realized he was finished, Bella was kissing him, and handing him Marcie, a warm, squirming bundle of energy. He held on tight and she relaxed into his arms.

His brother, Bob, handed him an open bottle of cold beer. He looked at the label and read it out loud, "*Roaring Nora's IPA*. Never heard of that one." He gratefully swallowed a big gulp.

"You made it!" said his Dad.

"Really?" he said, in disbelief.

His Mom squeezed his shoulder from behind. "So glad you are okay," she said.

He knew it was impossible for him to have finished the Fun Run, but he remembered what John had said about the time stretching to hold the miles if you had enough heart, and he knew that he had really finished. He had outrun both a mountain lion and his fears.

## Danger Beyond The Yellow Gate

"Where's your pages?" asked laz.

Danger handed the bag over to him, and the pages were counted and all the checkpoints were accounted for, as he knew they would be.

"Congratulations," said laz, and held out his hand to Danger.

Danger shook his hand and smiled a weary smile.

Someone pushed a red and white button at the gate, and he heard a recording play, "That was easy."

"No, it most definitely was not," said Danger, laughing a bit.

Frozen Ed came over to shake his hand. "Good job, Danger!"

"Thanks. How did you do, Ed?" asked Danger.

"I made two loops; I finally did it again after all these years!" said Ed, smiling.

"Congratulations!" said Danger, happy for his friend.

He asked if anyone else was still in the race, but he already knew about Amanda, Emily, and Sam. He found out Frank and Mark had still not come in from Loop One, and there were several others struggling out there.

*Taps* was played by laz, a sad and cranky rendition with many missed notes. Danger stood at attention by the gate, with Marcie standing next to him, holding each other's hands and absorbing the notes.

Others came up to him and shook his hand, and said congratulations, then meandered away back to their campsites. Danger picked up Marcie, and she wrapped her chubby legs around his waist. He remained standing at the yellow gate, gazing down the road towards the bathhouse. There, a flash of blue—he thought he saw them! There was Clyde out in front, hands behind his back, followed by Harry and John. Harry lifted one hand in greeting.

Marcie said, "Dada," and he looked down at her precious head, happy to hear her little voice. He kissed her cheek, then looked up again. They were gone. Totally gone. Harry, John, and Clyde had vanished into the looming darkness of the evening.

Harry's words echoed in his mind, "When you don't need us any more, we will disappear."

He went to sit by the fire and stare into the flames, and Marcie sat in his lap pulling on his beard. Bella came and took her from him. "Let's go play with Gramma and Aunt Bibi," she crooned.

## Danger Beyond The Yellow Gate

His Dad hovered about, laying more logs on the fire, and sparks flew. Smoke wafted out and up. It was a clear night of endless stars above the campground.

laz, scRitch, Frozen Ed, his Dad, and his brother Bob all sat with him around the fire, eager to hear his stories. He thought about telling them about Harry, John, and Clyde, but something held him back. Perhaps that was just for him. Nobody would believe him anyway. He might tell Bob about it later.

He talked instead about the long days and nights of running up and down the hills, and how he didn't think he could finish. He talked about how his faith had gotten him through it, and he had been able to overcome adversity. He told about falling down and hitting his head on the first loop, the awful briars, the dog attack, the ticks, the wild boar, and the fearsome mountain lion. The others listened solemnly, and murmured platitudes.

scRitch handed him a piece of freshly cooked chicken, and he dug in hungrily, savoring every juicy morsel of flesh.

As he chewed, he looked around at the faces by the fire, and he thought he noticed a slight resemblance between laz and John, and between his Dad and

Harry. "Nah," he mumbled, and kept eating.

laz told him it was too bad he didn't finish all five loops. But if he went home and thought about it for a while, he might find the determination to come back and do all five. He wouldn't be a failure forever.

But Danger knew he didn't fail. He had never admitted defeat. He knew in his heart that he would come back, and he hoped he would see his friends out there once more.

**Never The End**

Made in the USA
Lexington, KY
04 June 2018

Made in the USA
Lexington, KY
04 June 2018